ALAN'S
CROSS-DRESSING
STORY

by

A. J. BETHELL

Introduction

This tale is based on a young man's life who believes he is alone with a strange problem. Alan has no idea that there are others like him and that there is even a name for those that do what he does.

This young man has convinced himself that if others discover his secret, he will be locked up as a pervert. Leaving his job to take care of his mother, his stress slowly rises, and he has to do something.

A female friend tries to convince the boy that there is nothing wrong with him and that he should tell his mother and sisters.

However, this young man is sure his family will want to get rid of him and eventually tries to do away with himself.

Eventually, the boy's friend changes his mind, and the young man tells his family.

The friend was wrong. Alan is banished from his family and has to be cared for elsewhere.

Alan's story spreads over a lifetime, but the account's timeline has been shortened to maintain interest.

It is hoped that the story means something to others as it has to Alan and his friends.

©Copyright 2022 A. J. Bethell

ALAN'S STORY

CHAPTER ONE

The boy with brown wavy hair had just turned eighteen. He didn't look eighteen. Alan was short and thin for his age. All the boy's friends were expecting a celebration party, but Alan didn't want a fuss.

After his tea that evening, the boy decided that he would take a walk to the local pub. The Squirrel public house was five minutes from his home, and the boy soon arrived.

The pub was quiet that night, and he knew that his friends would be at the Elm Tree, where loud music played most nights.

It wasn't that Alan didn't like loud music. On the contrary, he did and was often reprimanded for having his music too loud in his bedroom.

Alan had drunk one pint of bitter and was about to purchase a second when.

"Happy birthday, Alan." The boy turned and saw his neighbour, Susan Browning, standing before him and smiling.

The woman was in her mid-twenties, pretty with black shoulder-length hair and a cute little twist to her upper lip, giving her a permanent smile. Her cheeks glowed with the pleasure of seeing the young man.

"What can I get you, Susan?" So said the young man.

"I should be buying you a drink, Alan. After all, it is your birthday."

Alan insisted and then bought the woman a glass of sweet white wine. After handing her the glass of wine, Susan said:

"Shall we sit at a table?" The young man looked about the bar, there were plenty of empty tables, and the pair decided on the corner table near the window.

The two friends sat in silence and sampled their drinks, then the hum of traffic going by could just be heard.

"Alan, I wanted to thank you for your help last week. I got a bonus for the extra work, and it was all down to you."

"I was glad to help. It got me out of the house, and you and your sister always have the place nice and quiet."

"Is that the only reason you offered to help me?"

"It was at first. Don't get me wrong. I don't crave peace and quiet. I love going to the Rock and Roll club once a month. The music is loud there, and I love it, but sometimes it's nice to be able to talk or hear yourself think."

"What about now? Do you still come over for the piece and quiet?"

"Not really; I like you and Beryl. You are always nice to me, and you listen when I talk. I know I go on a bit, but I can't talk to my family like I talk to you two." Susan stood, and Alan started to follow.

"No. You stay there. I'll get us another drink." Susan started for the bar when what looked like a beginner Punk Rocker entered the bar.

"I'll have whatever Alan is drinking." The barman was about to expel the young newcomer, but the landlord stopped him. The man using a low voice, said:

"Beryl's okay."

Susan bought the drinks, and the two sisters went and joined Alan at the table. The three friends chatted happily. Beryl had purchased a round of drinks, and Susan had bought another.

"It must be my round now," Beryl said:

"This is your birthday treat."

The three people in the corner seat saw the pub filling up as they drank their drinks. Then, Susan said:

"Why don't we go for a meal? The San-Pan has opened now, so we can try *their* meals."

Alan removed his wallet from his jacket pocket and checked to see what he had available, but Susan said:

"This is my treat. My bonus will cover it." Then Beryl chipped in.

"Our treat. I'll pay half."

The boy's face was glowing, but the girls said nothing. They drank their drinks, returned their glasses, and Alan helped the girls on with their coats, and they left The Squirrel Public House.

The meal at the San-Pan was good, and then the three caught the bus back home, stopping at the pub for one last drink.

In the col-de-sac, Susan said:

"Have you enjoyed your birthday, Alan?"

"It's been brilliant. Thank you both for a great night." Beryl asked.

"Will you be over tomorrow to help Susan to fill those envelopes?"

Alan looked a little guilty as he said:

"Not tomorrow. After work, I should join my friends for a drink. They were all looking forward to a party, and I have deprived them of that. I'm sorry, Susan. If you still want me to, I'll be over the next night?"

"Beryl kissed the young man on the cheek and went inside her house. Susan kissed Alan full on the mouth, something she had never done before, and then she said:

"I'll see you then. Don't have tea when you get home; I'll cook you something myself." Alan blushed again, which got him another kiss, then the friends departed to their respective homes.

Alan was still stroking his cheek as he entered the back door of his home. His mother was just putting the kettle on for a cup of tea.

"She's kissed you then?" Alan flushed again, then answered his mother.

"Yes, she did. She kissed me on the lips." Alan's mother didn't want to embarrass her son and left the subject there.

"Tea! Alan?"

"Yes, please, mum."

Mother and son sat in the lounge and drank their drinks. Alan told his mother what a great evening he had had and that he was going out the next night with his mates to not disappoint them.

In bed that night, Alan was restless. The boy had wrestled with a secret for a long time. That night had brought everything back to the forefront of his mind.

Alan wanted to tell someone his secret but wondered what the consequences would be. Alan struggled with his thoughts and found it challenging to get to sleep.

The boy eventually got off to sleep, but the sleep was interrupted by nightmare dreams.

Six o'clock the following morning found the young man still tired but making tea and starting breakfast.

"Morning, Alan. I'll just drink my tea, then while you make your lunch, I'll finish cooking the breakfast."

At first, that morning at work, Alan was having difficulty concentrating. But, by lunchtime, he was feeling better. Then, Martin, his friend he had known since primary school, looked in.

"You ready for tonight? Alan?"

"Yeah, of course. We'll meet up at the Elm Tree and start from there." Martin left the office, and Alan smiled to himself.

It was going to be a great night. Sink a few pints at the pub, then off to the Rock and Roll club and a Chines meal at the San-Pan. Thanks to Susan and Beryl, he now knew what the food was like.

Alan arrived home, and his mother said:

"There's plenty of hot water for your bath, Alan. Do you want a sandwich before you go out, or would you like something cooked?"

"Just a sandwich, please, mum." He said over his shoulder as he mounted the stairs to the bathroom.

Half an hour passed when.

"Your sandwich is ready and on the table, Alan. I'm going over to Susan's for a chat, and I'll give her a hand with her envelope job." Alan called back a thank you and then said:

"It's called 'envelope stuffing,' mum."

"That sounds horrible, Alan." But the boy assured his mother that that was what everyone called it.

Soon, Alan was checking himself in the full-length mirror by the front door. Hair neatly styled in the Teddy Boy fashion. Sharp crease in his tight trousers and his long Edwardian jacket spotless, with a white handkerchief in the breast pocket.

Alan opened his jacket to look at the new red and gold waistcoat he had recently bought. Adjusting his bulls-head bootlace tie, the young man was happy with his appearance.

Alan ate his sandwich, quickly washed up, and then cleaned his teeth before calling at Susan Browning's house. It was Susan who answered the boy's knock.

"Hi Susan, can you let my mum know I am off now and I'll see her later."

"I will, Alan, and you look great." Susan then kissed her neighbour on the cheek, and Alan left for the Elm Tree.

CHAPTER TWO

Martin raised his glass as Alan entered the bar. Some of his friends, some with girls hanging on their arms. The music was loud, and there was a party atmosphere.

"Over here, Alan!" Called Eric Simpson, the landlord of the Elm Tree.

The man handed the young man a pint of bitter and said: Here's your first legal pint in 'The Elm Tree.' Alan blushed.

"They've just told me. Anyway, happy birthday."

"Thanks, Eric. And thank Lilly for me." The young Teddy Boy joined his friends then the group left to hear their beloved Rock and Roll.

Alan enjoyed his evening. He avoided having too much to drink, and the meal was just as good as the previous night.

After the San-Pan, everyone walked part way to their individual destinations, and they sang some of the rock and roll songs. Then, they sang happy birthday to Alan three or four times before they dispersed.

Alan arrived home to find two suitcases in the entrance hall.

"Mum! I take it; Janet and Eleanor are home?"

"They arrived about an hour ago. There is a couple of presents for you in the lounge."

"I'll wait till morning, mum. The girls can watch me open them."

The woman ruffled her son's hair like he was a little boy and said:

"You're a good boy, Alan. You never cause me any problems. Your sisters were always bringing trouble home when they were your age."

Alan grinned and hugged his mother. Then the woman said:

"I wasn't going to say anything, but your gift from me is also in the lounge."

"I'd like to wait until the morning, mum. If you don't mind."

Alan took himself to bed. He had missed his sisters, but those thoughts would be more potent now that they were home from their holiday.

Alan carefully removed his shoes and suit in his room, hanging his suit on the outside of his wardrobe to air before stowing it away until it was needed again.

Alan then put on his pyjamas, laid on his bed with his hands under his head, and closed his eyes.

The boy now pictured his twin sisters, whom he hadn't seen for six weeks while they travelled in America.

The boy visualised the two girls who always dressed the same. He could see them sitting at the kitchen table in the morning, waiting for him to open his gifts.

Alan contemplated his problem. Who could he talk to? Things were getting worse, and the boy's mind was in turmoil.

Sleeping little that night, Alan decided to get up earlier than usual.

Quietly, the young man descended the stairs. Then closing the kitchen door almost silently, the boy made himself a pot of tea.

Alan was still at the table when his mother entered the room at six o'clock.

"What's the matter, Alan. Can't you sleep?"

"I don't know why, mum, but I can't."

"Do you want a cooked breakfast like usual? I'll have to close the door if you do. I don't want to wake the girls too early."

"I'll just have cereal today, mum. Thank you."

"What did you want?"

"I'll get it, mum. Can I get you something?" Then, feeling the pot on the table, Alan's mum said:

"I'll make some more tea." The woman closed the kitchen door, put the kettle on, emptied the pot, rinsed it with hot water, and prepared it for another round of tea.

Alan had finished his cereal, and his mother was just about to pour another cup of tea when the kitchen door opened, and a pair of girls said:

"We'll have a cup of tea if there is still one in the pot?" The girls held the gifts before them. Janet placed two on the kitchen table, and Eleanor had the other one.

Alan took the parcel that had his mother's writing on it. The package was soft, and the boy had no idea what was inside.

Carefully opening the gift so as not to tear the paper, Eleanor said:

"Just rip the paper, Alan. You always open packages like a girl."

"Not like this girl." So said Janet with her index finger pressed to her chest. Everyone laughed.

Alan got the paper off the gift, unfolded the satin material to find a blue satin waistcoat with Buddy Holly, and Elvis embroidered, one on each side and a record depicting the name 'Heartbeat.' On one and 'Jailhouse Rock.' on the other.

"It's brilliant, mum." The boy stood and hugged his mother. "I'll wear it under my suit today."

The two girls, in unison, cried out.

"Open mine next!"

"Alan can only open one at a time, girls."

Eleanor's gift was opened first. Alan found a Bill Haley record that was made into a clock." Eleanor said:

"I thought that it would look good on your bedroom wall."

Alan stood again, kissed his sister, and thanked her for the marvellous present. Alan couldn't wait to see what Janet had managed to get him.

"I wish I could wear this tie to work today; Martin would be so jealous." The boy showed the tie with a piano keyboard down one edge and a picture of Fats Domino at its widest point.

Janet got her hug and kiss from her brother. Each apologised to the young man for not parting with their gifts sooner.

Alan said that he understood. The boy's sisters were thousands of miles away, and as his mother said:

"I wanted you to receive all our presents together." Alan was about to leave for work, and his sisters said they wanted to take their young brother for a meal at lunchtime. So naturally, the boy assented to the offer.

At work that day, Martin was impressed by the embroidered blue satin waistcoat. However, the office manager frowned and said:

"I hope this won't be repeated tomorrow, young man."

"It won't, Mr. Clarke. It's just that it was a present for my birthday from my mother."

"Very fashionable, I'm sure. Now you had better keep your jacket button. Mr. Saunders will not be happy."

Alan thanked the man for his kindness, then fastened his jacket buttons and continued with his work.

Lunchtime arrived, and Alan went out the door to the High Street, and coming along the path were his sisters. Both dressed in green pleated skirts, wide black leather belts, and white frilly-fronted blouses. The day was fine and sunny, so neither girl wore a jacket or cardigan.

Alan stood by the door to the offices and watched his siblings approach. Alan watched their skirts as they swung from side to side.

The meal was held in the small public house opposite the offices where the young man worked.

The boy ended up sitting between his sisters, declining a beer and accepting a lemonade. Alan got a glimpse of the girl's frothy petticoat ends as the girls sat down. And he felt a strange tingling rush through his body.

That afternoon after the meal, Alan tried hard to concentrate on his work, but his mind was elsewhere. Luckily, Martin went into the office several times to collect documents, and the boy's mind was distracted.

That evening after work, Alan was sitting on the bus; his mind was a jumble of thoughts. Then, finally, the bell rang for his stop, but the boy never heard it and ended up several miles from his stop.

"Where have you been, Alan? Susan has been waiting for you."

"I got a bit behind, mum, and I missed my bus. So I'll go over to Susan's now."

Alan walked straight across the road to his friend's house and knocked.

"Hello, Alan. I was really worried about you."

Alan gave Susan the same story that he had given to his mother, and then in the kitchen, Susan, Beryl, and Alan ate chicken pie and chips, with apple pie and cream as a dessert.

"I'm off to see Sarah. Don't wait up." Susan said:

"Aren't you going to put all that make-up on tonight?"

"No. I think I'm past that fashion." Alan told Beryl she looked much nicer as she was. "Don't wash up; I'll do it in the morning."

Beryl was then out of the house.

"Are you feeling alright, Alan? You look strange tonight."

"I'm fine. Let's get on stuffing these envelopes. I want to try and get you another bonus."

Alan was quiet as he worked and Susan kept glancing at the boy.

"Are you sure you want to help me?"

"Of course I do. Come on, your getting behind."

Working away together, the pair said little. Then Susan couldn't stand it any longer.

"Come on! You have something on your mind, Alan. What is it?"

The boy flushed and then said he couldn't talk about it. Susan said:

"Look, Alan. We have known each other for more than five years. You were here for me when Mick left. You were only thirteen then, but you helped me a lot. You helped with the garden, you helped me take rubbish to the tip and helped me when I was shopping. We even cleaned the house together. When your dad died, You slept over here for a few nights while your aunt came and stayed. So come on, you can tell me anything.

Alan shook his head.

"I can't tell you anything."

Susan got up, went to her sideboard, and removed two glasses and a bottle of brandy. Then, putting a generous measure into each glass, the young woman handed the boy a glass and told him to drink it down.

Alan coughed as he swallowed the warming liquid. Susan had sipped hers, then she replenished the young man's glass.

"Now, Alan. Talk to me. What you tell me will go no further; I won't even tell, Beryl."

Alan still shook his head.

Susan tried to reason with the boy but to no avail.

"Let's get on with our work." Said the boy, sitting back down to continue the job.

Susan watched as the boy inserted the various pieces of the order that had to go into each envelope. Susan was worried about Alan. Then she said:

"Should I have a word with your mum?"

"My mum knows nothing about what's wrong."

"So...There is something wrong?"

Alan had made a slip and had to admit that something was on his mind. Susan tried to make light of the situation.

"Have you robbed a bank?"

"Don't be silly."

"Well, have you stolen anything from anyone?"

"I don't steal, you know that."

"Look, Alan, I'm trying to help you. Have you done anything illegal, anything at all?" Alan's face turned red, and the boy held his head down in shame. The woman told, Alan that a problem shared is a problem, halved. Then.

"What…Have…Done…Alan?"

CHAPTER THREE

Alan just held his head down, and the boy's shoulders quivered. Susan placed her arm around the boy's shoulders and asked again.

"What have you done that is so bad, Alan?"

The boy started to breathe heavily. Then, finally, he sat himself up and asked.

"May we sit on the settee?"

"Of course, if that helps."

Alan sat on the settee, and Susan sat on the armchair opposite the young man.

"No, Susan. I want you to sit next to me. I don't want to look into your face."

"That ugly am I, now?"

"That's a ridiculous thing to say. No, you are beautiful. It is just that I can't say what I have to say if I can see your face."

Susan moved to the boy's side. Susan placed her hand on the young man's knee. "Please don't touch me. When you take your hand from me disgusted, it will make me feel even worse."

Susan was terribly worried now about her friend. What terrible thing was he about to impart to her. Now that the crunch had arrived, Susan wondered if she wanted to know Alan's secret. Then in a soft voice, the woman said:

"I'm ready, Alan, if you are."

Alan started to silently cry. Susan was about to embrace her friend but remembered what he had said.

Susan handed the boy a tissue. He wiped his eyes and took another deep breath.

"Susan. What I am about to tell you; started about six months after my dad died." The boy paused for nearly a minute, which seemed much longer to Susan. Then.

"When I was alone at home, I did something and have repeated it several times since, and I think I might have to be sent away to a special hospital for the insane." The young man was silent again but for a little longer this time. Susan started to break the silence.

"I'm sure…."

Alan stopped the woman by raising his finger to his lips.

The boy had to take another breath before he could continue.

"One day, when I was alone in the house. Mum, Janet, and Eleanor had gone to grans to help her. I, can cannot do this."

Susan told the boy, that he had now started and should continue.

Alan cried again. He pleaded with his friend, he told her that he didn't want to be taken away.

Susan took, Alan's hand in hers and told him that he needs to talk. Alone pause ensued before he said:

"I remember that it was raining so I couldn't go out. So, and I don't know why, but I went into Eleanor's room and looked in her wardrobe at her clothes. It could have been Janet's room, but it wasn't. Then I touched the dresses and skirts that hung before me; before I knew it, I had put on one of Janet's skirts. I had removed my trousers and was walking about the house in a skirt."

Susan put her arm around the boy's shoulders and squeezed him to her. Alan's tears were raining down onto his lap.

"I take it none of your family have been told?"

"I couldn't. Mum will have me sent away. I'm sick. I don't know how you can bare to touch me."

Alan stood to leave, but Susan held onto the boy.

"Did wearing Eleanor's skirt make you feel good?"

"Not at first. I felt sick and strange and soon removed it. I put it back exactly where I had found it; I even ensured it was facing the same way on the hanger."

"Have you done this much?" Alan nodded his head. Then in a whisper said:

"Yes, I have. I do it every time I'm alone in the house." Susan then asked the boy if that was why he didn't like being left alone at home.

"That's right. I'm afraid that mum or my sisters will catch me, and then mum will have to call the doctor, then I'll be taken away."

Susan poured out two more brandies before explaining to the young man by her side.

"First. You are not insane. There are a lot of men and boys just like you. Most keep their secret as you have been doing because, like you, they feel that what they are doing is wrong. Second, I think you should tell your mum and sisters. I know it won't be easy, but they should know."

"I can't do it. What about Eleanor. It's her clothes that I wear. I've often worn her green skirt that she and Janet like to wear, and I've worn the pink dress she bought on holiday a couple of years ago."

Susan asked if there were a particular time when the need to change clothes was greatest. The boy said that when things seemed tough or something changed.

"What about now?"

"Well, being eighteen isn't all it's cracked up to be. I have to move on to the next office soon, and I am happy where I am. I have to vote now, Mum tells me. And now, I am a legal adult and will be treated as such. Oh, there are a thousand things that now have to change with all the stress...I don't know. I can't just relax."

"For a start, you have a vote, but you don't have to use it. Now we have that little problem out of the way. Tell me. Do you feel stressed now?"

"Yes. Very."

Susan took the boy's arm and led him upstairs to her bedroom. Susan opened her wardrobe door, and many dresses were packed into the cupboard. Then opening the other door, Susan said:

"And here we have skirts."

Alan stared at the array of feminine clothing before him.

"You can touch them if you want to." Sheepishly the boy stepped into the feminine room and went to the great wardrobe. Then, Alan ran his fingers along the dresses and repeated the action with the skirts.

Alan was silent as he perused the array of clothes. Then he heard Susan's voice.

"Alan, have you ever worn knickers and a bra?"

Alan shook his head; the boy didn't know what to say. Finally, Alan was told to select a dress. The boy looked at the different styles and colours and chose a grey dress with a pleated skirt.

Susan lifted it from the rail and laid it on the bed.

"You'll need knickers, bra, slip, stockings, and suspender belt. I have a pair of sandals that will hopefully fit you. I'll leave you to get changed. If you need help with the bra, just call me. But you should be okay if you put it on back to front, then turn it round. It'll help with the stockings."

Alan was alone, staring at the clothes on the bed; he knew that he had to wear them, so he quickly removed his clothes. Then he put on the knickers. The satin was cool and smooth; at first, his penis started to stiffen. Alan remembered what Susan had said about the bra. He had the thing in place then pulled the slip over his head. The garment felt sensual as the soft fabric floated down his body to his knees.

"Susan!" The boy called.

Susan knocked on her bedroom door. Alan said:

"I've got as far as the slip."

Susan lifted the slip and found that Alan had the suspender belt around the wrong way. With care, the young woman righted the mistake, and she helped Alan on with his stockings, fastening them to the suspenders.

Alan also needed help pulling up the zip at the back of the dress. Then stepping into the shoes, Alan was now ready to venture back downstairs to the lounge.

"What if Beryl comes home early?"

"Don't worry about it, Beryl. She'll be okay."

Then Susan and Alan continued to fill the envelopes. Finally, Susan opened a bottle of wine, and soon the boy was light-headed.

Alan wanted to run and hide when the front door opened, but there was nowhere to go.

"Wait here."

Susan left the room. Alan listened to the voices waiting for the hysterical laughter, but none came. Then slowly, the door opened; Alan's heart was beating so fast he thought his chest would explode.

"Evening, Alan. I'm off to bed." So said Beryl without batting an eyelid.

Alan was still shaking when Susan returned to the room and carried on with the envelope stuffing.

"Would you like to stay the night, Alan?"

The boy was shocked by Susan's question. Then after some thought, Alan said:

"I'd better go home tonight. Mum will be worried I won't get to work on time."

Alan thanked the young woman, then apologised for not staying.

Alan went to Susan's bedroom and changed back into his male clothing. Alan had had a great evening but was still worried that what he was doing was wrong.

"Now, Alan, you must tell your mum about this."

"I can't. Not yet. Please, Susan, don't you say anything, will you?"

"I promise to say nothing, but you will have to speak to your mum at some point." Alan reluctantly agreed. However, the boy was convinced that he was doing something illegal, if not terribly wrong, although he felt good and relaxed when wearing Susan's clothes.

The pair kissed at the front door, then Susan, as they parted, said:

"Let's talk some more tomorrow. You will come over and help me again?"

Alan just said the one word.

"Yes."

The boy crossed the road to his home. Alan's mother was just opening the door as the young man arrived.

"There you are, Alan." The boy's mother waved to Susan.

"I nearly came over to let you know the time."

Alan went straight to the kitchen. He was going to make the late-night cuppa. His mother had made the tea, and their mugs were steaming on the table.

"Janet and Eleanor have had their tea and gone to bed."

Mother and son drank their tea in silence. Alan washed the mugs and put them on the mug tree.

"Are you alright, Alan?"

"Of course, mum. Why shouldn't I be?"

"It's just that you have been quiet for the last few days; I thought perhaps something was wrong at work."

"Everything is fine, mum."

The boy wanted to add. 'I promise.' But couldn't bring himself to lie to his mother.

CHAPTER FOUR

Laying on his bed that night, Alan remembered his evening with Susan. A smile played across the boy's lips, then he shuddered. Finally, to himself, he said:

'I really did wear that dress. I was with Susan and wore a dress. I think Beryl said nothing about me dressed as a girl.'

The boy's smile appeared again.

Before drifting off to sleep, Alan saw his mother's face. It was stern, and she was shaking her head.

Alan fell asleep with that image of his mother. Then during the night, he dreamt that he had told his mother his secret. She was angry, and she was pointing to the door. Janet was shouting at him, as was Eleanor.

A van pulled up at the front door, and he felt the straps tighten around his wrists as the two strong women in white coats dragged him from his home.

The boy's mother and sisters called him names and said he was disgusting.

"We don't want you back here, Alan. Even when you have been cured of your perversion."

Alan suddenly woke and sat bolt upright. He had been crying while asleep and his pillow was wet.

Alan decided that he had to keep his secret. The boy was determined to never wear a skirt or dress again.

The following morning at the breakfast table. Alan stared at his mother and sisters, then diverted his eyes away.

Alan found it challenging to converse that morning. Finally, the boy's mother said:

"What's the matter, Alan?"

"Nothing, mum. Just a bit tired, that's all." Eleanor whispered to Janet.

"I bet he's in love." The girls winked at each other and smiled.

That day at work, Mr. Clarke found the young man quieter than usual, as did Martin. Alan just repeated what he had said to his mother.

That evening, Alan just ate a slice of buttered toast before heading over the road to Susan's.

"Hello, Alan. Come in."

Alan stepped over the threshold and entered the hall.

"Shall we start on the envelopes, Susan?"

Susan was surprised at the boy's demeanour that evening.

Then the young woman said:

"Would you like to go and get changed first? I've put a skirt and blouse out for you." Alan declined the offer.

"I have decided to never wear any female clothing again. It was a mistake. I shouldn't have said anything to you. Please forget what I have told you and what I did last night." The boy paused before saying. "And can you ask Beryl to forget what she saw?"

Alan entered the lounge dining room and sat at the table, ready to start work.

"Are you alright, Alan? Last night you enjoyed wearing my dress."

"I must never do that again. I'm never going to put on a dress. That's girls' stuff, and I'm a boy. I knew I should have kept my mouth shut."

Susan was standing behind the boy, she rested her hands on his shoulders, and in her soft voice, she said:

"If you change your mind, no one will ever know. Not even your mum and sisters."

Alan didn't answer. He just picked up an envelope and started working.

Over the next few months, Alan's demeanour changed. Finally, the boy seemed happy and full of life. Most evenings, Alan could be found with Susan stuffing envelopes and enjoying the odd TV movie.

It seemed as though the boy had banished any thoughts of dressing in female attire.

Susan and her sister Beryl never mentioned that one night and everything seemed as it was before.

Alan was invited to holiday with his friend, Martin, and his family. They travelled to Cornwall and spent a week in a cottage.

Martin's sister was fun to be with, she liked to dance, and she sang in the talent competition, coming second and winning a cup and a large box of chocolates that she shared with the family.

During the second half of the week, Sally started wearing dresses or skirts, and Alan looked more closely at his friend's sister. Martin said:

"Do you fancy Sally or something?"

"No, course not. She's a bit young for me."

Alan realised that his friend had noticed him studying the girl, but it wasn't the girl he stared at but her clothes, which she wore so well.

Then on their return home, Alan found a long envelope waiting for him.

The young man opened the envelope and studied the contents.

"Everything all right, Alan?" Asked his mother.

"I'm to be moved to the other branch, mum. Those offices in the town centre."

"That means more money doesn't it, Alan? That will be marvellous."

"It means a lot more work though, and the work is more demanding."

Alan's mother was pleased for her son and asked when he had to start at the new office.

"In four weeks. I will be on the top floor."

Alan felt his stomach turn over at the thought, but the extra money would be handy.

Alan told Susan that evening, and the young woman was over the moon for her friend.

"let's go out and celebrate. We'll have a drink at The Squirrel and then onto the San-Pan for a meal. My treat."

"I'll go and change first."

Alan was soon back in one of his casual Jackets and grey trousers. The pair went to the pub, then to the restaurant, then back to Susan's.

"Beryl's out tonight. Would you like to stay?"

Alan was nervous at first, then Susan said:

"If you feel uncomfortable, you don't have to stay."

"I'd like to. As long as Beryl doesn't mind."

"She won't be here."

"And she won't mind me using her bed?"

Susan laughed, then said:

"You won't be using her bed. I want you to sleep with me."

Susan saw the colour drain from the boy's face.

"Does that horrify you?"

Alan found it hard to find his voice. Then slowly, he said:

"It was a bit of a shock when you said that."

Susan poured them a small glass of wine, and they sat and sipped their drinks. Then Susan dropped the bombshell.

"You've been thinking about wearing female clothes again, haven't you?"

At first, Alan felt faint. He was going to deny it, but he knew at the bottom of his heart that Susan could tell.

"I really don't want to dress up. I've been trying hard to keep those thoughts out of my mind."

"What's wrong?"

Alan explained about the new job promotion. The young man had to tell Susan that the job was a lot harder than he was used to and meant a lot more work.

As the couple sat in the lounge drinking. The telephone rang. Susan took the call.

"It's for you, Alan. It's Janet."

Susan listened to Alan's side of the conversation and watched as the boy's face became pained and strained. Silently the boy replaced the telephone receiver and turned to the young woman on the settee.

"My mum has been rushed to hospital. She fell down the stairs and has broken her leg, but Janet and Eleanor don't know anymore."

Susan said:

"You had better get to the hospital. I would run you in the car, but I have been drinking. I'll get you a taxi."

Susan called the taxi firm, and they arrived quickly.

Susan accompanied the young man.

They found Janet and Eleanor. They had been crying.

Alan thought the worst and expected his sister to say that his mother had died.

"Alan, Mum, has broken her leg, but she has also done a lot of damage to her hip."

"Can I see her?"

Janet told her brother that he could but not to expect much. Alan was horrified to see the state of his mother. She even had black eyes. The boy turned to the doctor and said:

"Did someone hit my mum?"

"No. The black eyes occurred when she hit her face when she arrived at the bottom of the stairs. Your mother will be alright, but she will need care. We will keep her here for a few weeks until we are sure everything is as it should be, and then she will come home. But she will need looking after."

Then the three siblings and friend had to leave the hospital. Susan arranged a taxi, and they travelled home. The twins went to pay the taxi driver, but Susan wouldn't hear of it.

Susan asked Alan if he wanted to stay the night. She assumed he would say no, but after looking at his sisters, who nodded to him, he accepted the offer. Then as he was about to cross the road with his friend, Janet said:

"Don't forget to take your clothes for tomorrow with you."

Alan soon arrived on the doorstep with a suit, shirt and clean underwear over his arm and folded, and out of sight were his pyjamas.

"See you tomorrow, girls." Alan then entered Susan's house."

The young woman told Alan that he could relax and unwind from his trauma tonight.

CHAPTER FIVE

A glass of brandy was placed into the boy's hand. Susan sat beside him. She saw the pyjamas and said:

"You won't need those tonight."

Alan blushed. He was going to sleep naked with this woman.

Alan sipped away at his drink, and soon his glass was empty.

Susan took the young man by the hand and started to lead him to the stairs; Alan put his hand out for his pyjamas.

"No. Not tonight, Alan."

Alan blushed again. Susan almost pulled the boy up the stairs to her bedroom. Then once inside.

"You can put your clothes on that chair."

Susan pointed to one of two chairs in the large bedroom. Alan had never been naked in front of any female before, except the doctor who gave him his last work medical. Alan was facing the wall as he removed his jacket and shirt, then his shoes and socks, finally slipping down his trousers and underpants. Alan heard a drawer open and close, then Susan said:

"I want you to put these on."

Alan turned his head and saw the naked Susan holding a pair of pink frilly knickers and a short pink nightie. The nightie was all satin and lace and, to Alan, looked like the sort of thing a young woman would wear.

Alan said nothing; he just took the knickers and slipped into them. Then pulling the nightie over his head, Alan felt a strange tingling in his body. He could feel his cheeks burning. Susan was also in pink. The night dress fell to her knees and was of satin, all shiny and slippery.

Susan pulled the quilt down from the bed from the pillows. Walked around the bed, took the boy by the hand, and led him to the bed.

The pair were silent as the young woman helped the young man onto the bed.

Alan had no experience with women, only as mates. This night was different. Alan could feel his insides quivering, and he was gently manoeuvred onto the bed.

Susan pulled the pink polka-dotted quilt over the boy, round to the other side of the bed the young woman climbed in beside her friend.

With the quilt over them, Susan snuggled into Alan, then put her arm around his neck and pulled him towards her.

"Relax, Alan. You're very tense." Alan started to speak, but his voice was gravelly. Then, after a slight cough, the boy said:

"I've never done this before." Then Alan closed his eyes.

"What haven't you done before? Worn a nightie or gone to bed with a woman."

"Both." Alan choked out.

Susan told the boy that he had to relax.

"No one will come in. Beryl is with her friend all night tonight. Janet and Eleanor are probably in bed right now, and you know your mum won't be here."

"I hope my mum will be alright?"

"Look, Alan, your mum is in the best place now. She'll be looked after. So all you have to do is relax. And I'm going to help you."

Susan started caressing the young man's chest with her free hand. Her hand slowly moved about Alan's nightie, and the boy found the sensation relaxing.

Alan moved closer to Susan as her hand moved down his body, and she smoothed his nightie around his stomach. Alan twitched, and Susan smiled at the boy.

"Would you like me to turn out the light, Alan?"

"I don't know. What's normal?"

"Both are okay, but I would prefer to see you enjoy your experience, but as this is your first time, I'll leave that up to you.

Bashfully, Alan said:

"You can leave the light on."

Susan nodded then; with one hand, she threw the quilt from the bed, and the pair lay motionless for a moment. The young woman let Alan take a breath, then, kneeling beside his prone body, Susan started to massage the boy's chest and stomach simultaneously.

Alan tried to keep still, but the sensation made him twitch and squirm.

Moving her right hand down from the boy's stomach, Susan ran her hand over Alan's genitals; she felt his penis stiffen. Alan's face burned.

Susan moved herself to a better position, lifted the boy's nightie, placed her hand on his knickers, and let it lie there.

Alan was afraid to move. The boy could feel the throbbing of his genitals, and he knew that Susan could too.

Leaving her right hand where it was on Alan's knickers, Susan took Alan's hand with her left hand and placed his hand on her breast.

"Caress it, Alan."

Alan wasn't sure what to do, but as gently as he could, he moved his hand about the woman's breast. Susan closed her eyes and gave a little moan.

"Keep your hand there, Alan."

Susan then slipped her hand inside the boy's knickers and took hold of his testicles. Alan could feel his penis becoming erect. His mind was a whirlwind of feelings, fear, and excitement. Then suddenly, The boy felt his knickers being pulled down his legs, and Susan bent over his genitals, gently taking the young man's stiff penis; she placed her lips over the head of his hard phallus, and Alan watched as the thing disappeared into her mouth.

Susan moved her head up and then down until Alan ejaculated. Then, Susan lifted her head, and Alan saw sperm dribbling from the side of her mouth.

"Pass me a tissue, Alan."

The boy took the small box of paper tissues from the bedside cabinet, and Susan wiped her mouth. Alan was breathing heavily as the young woman asked.

"Was that nice, Alan."

"It was fantastic, Susan. I've never felt like that before."

Susan removed her nightie and laid back on the bed. Alan started to remove his night dress, but Susan told him to keep it on.

"Put your knickers back on as well. Then I want you here."

The woman then patted the bed next to her.

Alan was then instructed to caress the girl's breasts, and she moved his hands down her body until he had reached every part. Susan moaned with the pleasure of his delicate fingers, and soon they were both exhausted.

"Look at the time, Alan. You had better get some sleep."

"You won't tell anyone about me wearing a nightdress, will you?"

"Alan, your secret is safe with me. I won't even say anything to Beryl. I shan't tell her you stayed here tonight. Now get some sleep."

It was then that Alan realised how tired he was and soon he fell asleep in the arms of that wonderful woman.

CHAPTER SIX

A loud ring ringing woke Alan. Then Susan rolled over and pressed the button on the alarm clock.

"You wash and dress Alan, and I'll make us some breakfast."

Alan then saw himself in the long mirror on Susan's bedroom wall. Aloud, the boy said:

"So I really did wear a nightie."

"Yes, you did, Alan. I hope you enjoyed it as much as you appeared to do."

"I did, Susan. And thank you."

Susan tied the belt of her dressing gown tightly around her waist and went to the kitchen.

Alan was soon dressed and ready for work, and when he entered the kitchen, Susan saw that he was holding the nightie and knickers he had worn.

"I wasn't sure where to put these." He held up the nightie and knickers.

"Just pop them in the machine. I have washing to do later."

Susan and Alan sat at the kitchen table and ate their bacon and eggs. Alan made the tea.

"Beryl, not home yet?" Asked the young man.

"No. She'll just go straight to work."

As they cradled their warm mugs, Alan said:

"Did you mean it last night? You said you wouldn't say anything about me and the nightie."

"I promised, didn't I?"

That day at work, Alan was on air. He worked hard and got praise from Mr. Clarke.

Martin found Alan unusually cheery.

"You look like you've won a prize."

"I haven't, but I feel guilty about how I feel. My mum's in hospital. I should be sad."

Martin wanted details of Alan's mum's accident and wanted to know what was making his friend happy.

"That, my friend, is a secret. But, one day, I might tell you."

Martin shrugged his shoulders and left the office. Just before lunchtime, Mr. Clarke handed Alan a note. And he said:

"I have just heard about your mother. I hope she recovers quickly."

The boy thanked his boss and read the note. Janet and Eleanor wanted to meet Alan for lunch.

Alan was waiting in the pub opposite his office building. He was a little worried as to why they wanted to meet up.

Alan had found a table near the pub's window; he could see over the frosted glass bottom. He saw the two young women as they approached the pub. Like always, they looked identical. The girls were wearing the same floral patterned sundresses and short white cardigans.

As the girls entered, Alan stood to get them a drink, but they both waved him back into his seat.

Alan waited for the girls to get their drinks and arrive at the table.

"We've ordered some sandwiches, Alan." And like always, the girls spoke in unison.

"We have spoken to mum this morning. She's still in a lot of pain, but she is alright."

"Can we see her later?" The girls said that they could. Then Eleanor said:

"Janet is finishing work early today. She wants to get a few things from home for mum."

"Like what?"

"Oh, you know, nighties and some underwear. Mum also wants her slippers." Janet then interrupted.

"She won't be doing much walking for a while." Then Alan said:

"Shall I get mum some grapes or something?" Again in unison, the girls said:

"Not grapes, but some fruit would be nice." Alan then said:

"I'll see if Mr. Clarke will let me off early today to pick the fruit up. Shall I go home, or do I go straight to the hospital?"

"You can go straight there if you want to. Then, we can all travel home together."

The three of them ate their sandwiches as they chatted about their mother. They wondered what they would do when she came out of the hospital. Then, finally, they all had to return to work. The girls went off to the boutique, and Alan crossed the road. The young man watched as his sisters walked briskly along the high street to their place of work. He studied their dresses as they swung from side to side.

"What are you staring at?"

It was Martin. He grinned at his friend and continued.

"Was that Janet and Eleanor?"

"Yeah. We had lunch together. Sorting out what to do about mum."

"You have any news yet? Mind you, I suppose it's early days yet."

Alan explained to his friend as they climbed the stairs that his mother was still in a lot of pain, but she was alright in herself.

"Give your mum my regards when you see her." Then Martin continued up another flight of stairs to where he worked.

Alan asked Mr. Clarke if it was possible to leave a little earlier that day, and he gave his reason for asking. His wish was granted, and when the time came, the young man went off to the greengrocers and bought fruit and a bunch of flowers for his mother.

As the boy sat on the bus, he thought about that previous night. That nightie was good to wear. It was better than his pyjamas. He also hoped that Susan would keep to her word and that she would tell no one what he had done.

"HOSPITAL, MAIN ENTRANCE!" Called the conductor. Alan had time to get off the bus without rushing.

The bus was to remain at the hospital for fifteen minutes. Alan walked from the bus terminal, and as he did so, he watched a group of girls as they left the hospital. The girls wore red gingham dresses, and the young man tried to imagine himself wearing such a dress.

The boy had to shake his head to rid himself of the thought.

Alan arrived at his mother's ward just as his sisters did so.

The siblings' mother was pleased to see her children, they all chatted, and they were thanked for bringing along her things and the fruit and flowers.

"That was Alan's idea." Said the girls together as they usually said things.

Their mother's doctor came and spoke with them just before visiting was over.

The man explained that their mother would be in hospital for about six weeks, and if everything turns out alright, she will be allowed to go home.

"However, your mother will need someone to look after her." The doctor looked from girl to girl. Then Eleanor spoke alone.

"Would you, Alan be able to look after mum while Janet and I work? You must be owed holiday, especially by then."

"I'm afraid she will need looking after for more than a week or two."

Their mother put her hand out to her children.

"Don't worry, we'll sort something out."

The two girls and Alan left their mother sitting up in bed, waving to them as they walked out of the ward door.

"Are you going over to help Susan tonight?" Asked the girls.

"I expect so. If you don't need me to help you." The girls were happy for their brother to go to their neighbour's house; they knew he helped her with her job.

At home, the young man changed from his office suit and wore casual trousers and his shirt.

"Come in, Alan."

The young woman was pleased to see her friend, and after finding out how the boy's mother was, the couple started to fill the envelopes.

"Beryl's got some overtime at work, So I told her I would leave dinner until she got home. Have you eaten, or can I get you a snack to tide you over?"

"I'm fine, thank you. I'll wait. If I'm invited, that is?"

Susan laughed and told the young man he was invited to stay for dinner. Then as the pair worked away, Alan said:

"Do things work out alright for you and Beryl?"

"How do you mean, Alan. Work out."

"Well, you stay at home all day, and Beryl works. Doesn't she ever want to stay at home while you work?"

"Alan. I do work. What do you think we are doing now. I know you help me in the evenings sometimes, but I also do this all day. I also keep the house clean, wash and iron, and ensure that Beryl always has a hot meal in the evenings. We're both happy with this arrangement."

Alan was contemplating something; he was silent as he worked, then Susan broke the silence.

"Why do you ask?"

"I think Janet and Eleanor want me to stay home when mum leaves the hospital. They both have well-paid jobs and know I'm due some leave, but what I'm allowed isn't long enough to look after mum."

"Would the girls agree to you giving up your job?"

"I don't know. Mum's cleaning job isn't very well paid, but mum enjoys being with her friends, and the money is useful."

After a long pause, Susan snapped her fingers.

"I have an idea. If your sisters agree for you to stay home, I can ask if there is more work like this. You'll have to register for tax, but I can help you with that. We can work together. The amount you help me gets me a bonus; well, you might as well earn money in your own right. Part of the day, I'll come over and help you. Then you can make sure your mum is alright. Then you can come and help me. Your sisters don't go out very often, but I'm sure they will look after your mum some evenings."

Susan was getting excited about having her friend at home more often.

CHAPTER SEVEN

Well, time moved on, and it had been agreed that Alan would work from home. So the young man gave his notice to Mr. Clarke.

"I understand, Alan, why you want to leave, but are you sure."

"I am, Mr. Clarke."

"Well, I shall certainly miss you, young man."

Alan worked the rest of the month, and on his last day, the young man received a cheque for an extra two weeks' wages by way of a bonus.

The sibling's mother wasn't due to come home for another couple of weeks, so Alan got things ready for her. But unfortunately, the young man had been told that his mother wouldn't be able to manage the stairs. So her bed would have to be brought downstairs.

Alan carefully selected one of Eleanor's dresses. The dress was plain grey; it looked a little like a school dress; he removed his trousers and shirt, put the dress on, and then all alone, the boy had dismantled his mother's bed and taken it to the lounge. The bed was a little more challenging to put back together, but after a struggle, he managed it. Alan was going to have to have some help rearranging the furniture.

Alan looked at the mantle clock and discovered that his sisters would be home shortly, and then in a panic, he had to return the dress he had borrowed and put his trousers and shirt back on.

Alan had the kettle on for tea as the girls entered the house.

"I'm doing chicken pie and chips for dinner. I hope that's alright with you two.

The girls were glad they didn't have to cook again that night.

The young man made the tea, and the three drank their Beveridge in the kitchen together.

The girls went to change their clothes and were soon ready for their chicken pie meal.

Alan also gave the girls dessert and did the washing up.

"We're off out tonight, Alan. Will you be going over to Susan's?"

"Well, I was hoping to, but I need a hand with the lounge furniture. I was hoping that you could give me a hand to get the settee up to mum's room before you went out. It's in the way with mum's bed down here."

After much persuasion, Janet took the cushions upstairs, and Eleanor helped her brother with the settee.

"Look at the state of us, Alan. We'll have to change again."

Alan saw the girl ascend the stairs, they were a little moody, but the young man could understand their mood. Then as the young man started to the back door, the exit and entrance he used mostly, he heard his sisters arguing. This was something they *never* did, and this made Alan return to the foot of the stairs and listen.

Eleanor was accusing Janet of going into her room and touching her things. Janet told her sister what she thought of the accusation and how ridiculous it was.

"My clothes are the same as yours. We even take the same size, so why would I touch anything of yours?"

'My God.' Thought, Alan. 'I didn't put Eleanor's dress back exactly as I had found it.' Alan was sure he had, then realised that he may have made a mistake in his haste.

Alan left the house as quietly as possible and went to Susan's place.

"You look a little flushed, Alan. Is everything alright?"

"Yes, of course. Why shouldn't it be?"

"No reason, I suppose."

Alan knew that his friend guessed there was something, but as a friend, he knew she wouldn't push the issue, and then the conversation ended.

"Wine or tea, Alan?"

"I'd like a glass of wine, please."

Susan poured the drinks, and the two friends set to work on the envelope stuffing.

"Is everything ready for your mum's return?"

"More or less. I've got mum's bed in the lounge, and the girls helped me get the settee into mum's bedroom."

Beryl stuck her head around the door to let her sister know that she was off out.

"Hello, Alan. Bye." The young woman had gone.

"Don't you ever want to go out in the evenings, Susan?"

"I enjoy being in your company, and we have had a few nights out. I like the quiet life."

"You still haven't mentioned...You know what?"

"Don't keep worrying, Alan. I said I wouldn't say anything, and I haven't. However, I still think you should let your mum know about your feelings and needs. They are needs, you know, and not wants."

"Let mum get home from the hospital first."

After an hour or so's working, Susan said:

"Would you like to stay again tonight?"

Alan blushed. Then he remained silent for some time before saying.

"I really would like to, Susan, you know that. I haven't been able to get that night out of my mind. But Beryl will find out this time. I know she will."

"Beryl never gets home before midnight, and we will already be in bed. So in the morning, just get up early and get dressed. I'll have breakfast on the go by seven. If Beryl says anything, I'll tell her we worked on it, and I suggested you stay the night. She won't know that you slept in a nightie."

"I'll have to think about it."

The friends continued to work away. Then after he had had a think, the boy said:

"I'll go and leave a note for Janet and Eleanor. They might wonder what's happened to me."

Pushing an envelope and pen towards Alan. Susan said:

"Tear off the front and write on this envelope."

Alan's message was short and to the point. 'STAYING AT SUSAN'S TONIGHT.' Under the message, Alan printed his name and included an X.

The couple had worked hard that evening, and the envelopes had piled up. Alan put the bundles into the sacks while Susan made a nightcap of hot chocolate.

At about a quarter to eleven, the tired workers mounted the stairs to Susan's bedroom, where Alan was given another nightie to wear. The lilac nightie was covered in little hearts, and mauve ribbons tied into little bows adorned the garment. Like the first time, Alan had matching knickers to wear with his night dress.

Susan and Alan soon fell asleep, but Alan had a relaxed and contented smile as he slept.

The following morning when Alan woke, he noticed that Susan was missing. Then the boy looked at the clock on the bedside cabinet and saw that it was only six-thirty. At first, Alan lay there, then he pulled the quilt down, stared at the lilac nightie, and wondered why he felt so good. This also worried the young man, and he quickly removed the garment and dressed in his own clothes.

'I've got to stop all this.' The boy thought. 'I can't go on with this dressing up business.'

In the kitchen, Alan found Susan hard at work with the breakfast. Silently the young man sat down at the table; he watched as his friend checked the sausages and bacon as they sizzled away in the pan.

"I thought I could smell breakfast cooking." Beryl took the kettle, held it up like a trophy, and continued. "I'll make the tea, shall I?"

It was Susan who said that that would be good. Alan remained silent. Beryl had noticed the boy's silence and turned to face him. She said:

"Have a good night, Alan?" Then she winked at the young man.

Alan left his seat, then the house, and returned home to Janet and Eleanor, who were both at the kitchen table eating in silence. The boy was ashamed of what he had done. It was his fault that his sisters weren't talking to each other. Janet said:

"Do you want some breakfast, Alan?" Alan just shook his head and went to his bedroom, where he lay on his bed and wept.

'What have I done?" He asked himself. He never heard his sisters calling to him that they were off to work. He was fast asleep.

Suddenly the boy was woken by banging on the front door.

"Hello, Susan. What do you want?" The girl stared at her friend and then said:

"You've been crying. What's the matter?"

"You'd better come in."

Susan followed Alan to the lounge.

"There's not much room in here now, is there?"

"I haven't arranged things yet."

Susan offered to help Alan, and soon the place looked much better. The bookcase and the cupboard had been removed and were now in the boy's mother's bedroom.

Alan thanked Susan for her help, then he made a pot of tea, and the couple sat in the lounge. Susan just chatted away, then remembered what she wanted to tell Alan.

"I had a telephone call this morning from the Energetic Company. You have to go into town for an interview. Just telephone Mr. Stevens." Susan passed over the note she had written.

"Would you come with me, Susan? I'll call Mr. Stevens now."

After the call, it had been arranged that if Alan could be at the office by three, he would be interviewed.

Susan went to change her clothes, and Alan when and had a good wash and a shave and put on his best suit.

Alan then had his interview with Mr. Stevens of the Energetic Company.

CHAPTER EIGHT

As the young couple walked along the street, they chatted about Alan's job. Alan wasn't going to be stuffing envelopes, but he had promotional articles to pack into small boxes that had to be labelled and bagged for posting. The job had a slightly higher rate of pay than the envelope stuffing.

"I still want to come over to your place and help you. And I hope mum doesn't mind me using the garage and the shed."

"I'm sure she will be happy that you can earn a wage and be there to help her."

Susan and Alan decided to celebrate the young man's good fortune by going into the Bell public house for their afternoon tea. It was in the pub that Alan had something to tell his companion.

"I have inadvertently caused a rift between my sisters."

"What have you done, Alan?" The girl couldn't believe that Alan would do anything to upset his sisters.

"I borrowed one of Eleanor's dresses yesterday. I didn't want to, but as hard as I tried to resist the temptation, I needed to wear a dress more. I had the lounge to change and mum's bed to get downstairs. Then, there was the tea cook. And this morning, I decided that I would never wear female clothes again. Yesterday was going to be the last time. Janet and

63

Eleanor still weren't talking to each other this morning, and it's all my fault."

"You're not explaining yourself very well. What exactly did you do?"

"As you know, I have borrowed Eleanor's dresses or skirts from time to time. I told you I am always careful to put her clothes back exactly where I found them, even ensuring they are on the hangers the same way round."

"Yes, you told me about the trouble you go to."

"Well, yesterday I had forgotten about the time, and I had to rush and get changed before my sisters arrived home. Well, in my haste, I must have done something that made it clear to Eleanor that her clothes had been touched. Eleanor accused Janet of going into her room and touching her clothes. The two of them argued and aren't speaking to each other."

"Oh, Alan. You need to say something."

"I know I do. I wanted to say that I had touched the clothes last night but couldn't. So I came over to yours instead."

"So that was what was wrong. I said something was up, but you said nothing." Susan was upset that Alan hadn't confided in her.

"I was going to say something this morning to the girls, but when I found them still not talking, I was so ashamed that I took myself to my room. Then, I am ashamed to say, I cried myself to sleep. You woke me."

"We'll eat first, and then we'll go. When Janet and Eleanor return home, you need to talk to them. Then if you need to, come over to me."

The couple ate and then took the bus home. Susan kissed the young man, and she went indoors. Alan crossed the narrow street and let himself in the back door.

Eventhough, Alan wanted nothing to eat, he got a meal ready for his sisters, and while it cooked, Alan made a pot of tea.

The back door burst open, and two bedraggled women entered. Eleanor said:

"It's pouring with rain out there. I'm going to change before we eat." Janet said:

"Won't be long, Alan. Then we'll have tea."

The girls were still not talking. Alan now started to rehearse what he wanted to say. Over and over again, he said to himself.

'I'm sorry, Janet. I'm sorry, Eleanor. It was me who touched Eleanor's clothes.' Then he couldn't think how to continue. While he pondered his problem, the twins walked into the kitchen, laughing with each other. Janet then said:

"So what made you realise?"

When I took out my green skirt, then put it back because I had changed my mind about wearing it, the hanger caught the grey dress and unhooked one side. I don't know how but the dress hooked to the next hanger."

"So you thought it was me touching your stuff?"

"Yeah. Then as I thought about it. What does it matter anyway." The girls hugged each other and kissed. Then sat down at the table, and both in unison as was their wont, they said:

"So what's for tea, little brother?"

Alan quickly dished up the cottage pie and chips and said:

"I'll see you later."

Soon, Alan was with Susan, and as they stuffed the envelopes, Alan explained what had happened. The young couple laughed out loud.

"So, it wasn't your fault after all, Alan?"

"No, it wasn't. This has made me think, though. It could have easily been my fault, and my sisters would have hated each other."

"So you see, Alan. The time has come for you to be honest with your family. You can't go on like this. Your depression will worsen, and your need to cross-dress will become greater."

Alan was surprised at what Susan had called his problem.

"Is that a real name for what I have been doing, or did you make it up?"

Susan looked a little sheepishly towards the young man sitting opposite her at the table. Then, softly quietly, she said:

"Some time ago, I spoke to someone. I never mentioned you or your family. I needed to know what I could find so that I could help you. It was they who said that you were a cross-dresser or a transvestite. I think cross-dresser sounds nicer and sounds like what you are."

Alan was silent for a long time. Finally, the young man stuffed the envelopes, sealed them, bundled them, and filled the mailbag. Then Alan left the room.

"Are you alright, Alan?"

"I'm making some tea!" The boy called from the kitchen.

"Would you rather something stronger?" Alan wanted tea, and so they drank tea.

Susan waited and waited; she wanted Alan to say something or do something, but as time passed, the boy said nothing. Then, Alan said:

"I'd like a brandy if you don't mind."

Six mail bags were filled that evening. Not a record, but it was a lot. The pair drank their brandies, and Susan asked:

"Would you like to stay again tonight?"

"I had better not, Susan, but thank you anyway."

It was past eleven, and Beryl was still to return home.

"Would you like me to wait until Beryl is home? We can do a few more envelopes if you like?"

When Susan's sister arrived, the woman sensed something was up, but she had the tact to keep her mouth shut.

Alan kissed Susan on the cheek, and he left.

Susan soon began to worry that she had upset her friend, and that was something she hadn't wanted to do. A few days passed before the young woman was to have any news from her friend.

"Hi, Eleanor. Is Alan alright? I haven't seen him for a few days."

"I think the stuff has arrived for his job that you helped him get. There were loads of boxes in the garage, and Alan had tidied the shed. Go round and see him in the shed."

After thanking, Eleanor, the young woman ventured down the passageway that led to the back garden of Alan's house, and she found the boy at a bench filling little flat envelope-shaped boxes.

"Susan! What are you doing here?"

"I came to see if you were alright. You were so strange that night. I'm sorry if I offended you."

Alan stood up, took Susan in his arms, and kissed her. Then he said:

"Come in and see mum." Then walking through the open French windows into the lounge, Alan said:

"Mum, it's Susan. She's come over to see how we are. You two chat, and I'll make a drink."

Alan left the two women chatting. He could hear his mother praising him for what he had done and how he was looking after her.

"Here's your tea, ladies." Alan placed the little tray onto the small table by his mother's bed, then left to go to his shed.

"Alan has been a marvel, Susan. Look at what he has done for me; he cooks and cleans and has started this job of his. He's a lovely considerate boy."

"I know he is, Mrs. Berry."

"We've known each other for years now. Why don't you call me Sheila?"

Susan blushed before saying.

"It always seemed disrespectful somehow."

"Don't be daft. You're a friend and neighbour; you helped us out. Now call me Sheila."

"All right… Sheila. I'll try to remember."

After chatting some more, Sheila suggested that the young woman go and take Alan away from his work for a little while.

"Since those boxes arrived, Alan has been either out in the shed or attending to my needs. He needs a break from working."

Susan left the woman lying in her bed, and she went through the French windows to the shed.

"Your mum says that I should take you out for a while. I've been told you've been working hard since everything arrived, and we need to talk."

After locking his shed door, Alan went to his mother and checked that she would be alright for a while, and then Susan and Alan went for a walk.

"Martin is coming round tonight. Janet and Eleanor said they would stay with mum while I went to the Rock and Roll club. Did you want to come along? I can get you in as a guest?"

"Another time perhaps, Alan."

"You'll enjoy it. You never go out. I can invite two guests, so if you want Beryl to come along, I don't mind."

"Alan, you are avoiding talking to me."

"That's a silly thing to say. I am talking to you now. By the way, it's great the homework arrived so soon. Mr. Stevens said it wouldn't take long to get me started."

"Alan! Stop it."

Susan looked at the boy sternly. "Alan. I want to know what happened when you last came to my house. First, you didn't want to stay the night. That was fine, but you stopped talking to me, and when you left after Beryl had arrived home, you were strange. Now, what happened? I want to know if I said something that offended you."

Alan just walked by the woman's side; Susan could see he was deep in thought. Then slowly, Alan took Susan's hand in his and gently squeezed it. Finally, he stopped walking and looked about as if to check that they were alone. Then Alan said:

"I really did want to stay the night. That first night you made me feel fantastic. I had never experienced anything like that before. Wearing the nightie was amazing. That second time I felt so great wearing a nightie. I couldn't believe I could feel that relaxed just wearing such an item. You have been brilliant, and I could never thank you enough."

"I don't need thanking, Alan. I just want you to be happy."

"I am happy, Susan. However, after that last time wearing a night dress and what I thought I had done to my sister's I have decided that I never want to wear women's clothes again.

Susan and Alan started to walk again when Susan said:

"We can still be friends, can we?"

"Of course, we can. I'll still come over when I can and help you with your envelopes if you want me to. I just don't want to talk about...What did you call it?.. Cross-dressing anymore."

The couple walked to the park and once around the lake.

Alan kissed his friend and said:

"I have to get back. First, I need to prepare my sisters' tea and something for mum. Then I have to get ready for the club. Are you sure you don't want to come along?"

"You go and enjoy yourself with your mates, Alan. Will I see you tomorrow?"

"I'll help you tomorrow afternoon. Janet and Eleanor will be out tomorrow for awhile."

At the close, they parted, and Alan set to work with the tea.

"Alan!" Called the young man's mother. "Did you have a nice walk and chat with Susan?"

"Yes, mum. I promised her I would go over tomorrow afternoon and give her a hand. If you need me, you can telephone her, and I'll come straight back."

Alan was just putting the tea on the table as his sisters arrived home.

"We'll sort mum out, Alan. You had better have your bath and get ready."

After thanking the girls' Alan was soon in the bath, and by seven-thirty, Alan was ready in his suit with his hair all in place; then, there was a knock at the back door.

"Martin! Come in. I just have to see that mum is okay, and then we can leave."

Martin followed his pal to the lounge.

"Hello, Mrs. Berry. Are you feeling any better now?"

"I am, Martin, but it means a lot of work for Alan."

"I told you, mum, you're no trouble."

"Go will you, you two. Janet and Eleanor will be here to look after me. NOW GO!"

"Bye, mum!"

"Bye, Mrs. Berry!"

Two immaculate Teddy Boys strolled down the road to catch their bus. Susan had been watching from her kitchen window. She wanted to be with Alan. Unfortunately, the woman was falling in love with the young man.

CHAPTER NINE

Alan and his friends had a great night listening to their favourite music and downing a few beers. Every now and then, Alan would glance at the girls in their pretty dresses, then he thought about Susan.

The following afternoon, Alan was good to his word. After making sure his mother had everything, she needed, the young man went to help his friend.

Susan was glad that Alan had called over as he said he would. The two friends settled down to their envelope stuffing. The pair said little as they worked, except Susan asked Alan if he had enjoyed his night out.

"You should have come along with us, you know. We had a great time."

Susan smiled at the boy and told him she would go with him the next time if he wanted her to.

As they worked away, Susan wanted to talk to Alan about his cross-dressing, but she was afraid of upsetting her friend.

The afternoon wore on, and soon, Alan had to return home to check on his mother and get the tea ready.

"And I have a lot of work to catch up on."

Susan was worried that she was losing her friend. Alan was now busy with his work and looking after his mother and sisters.

Alan had stayed home for a few days. He wanted to get the job of packaging the sample boxes finished so that they would be ready for the van driver to collect them.

"Hello, Susan." Said Alan as the young woman came out to the van.

"Are you alright, Alan? I haven't seen you for nearly a week."

"Sorry about that, but I wanted to get that first assignment out of the way. Would you like me to come and help you later? Janet is staying home tonight."

"That would be really nice, Alan. I've missed you, you know. Please come and have tea with me tonight. Beryl will be out early."

"I'd like that. I'll let Janet know I'm having tea with you."

It had been settled, and Alan, after stowing away the new assignment and checking his mother, who had now started to sit up in an armchair. The young man took himself across the road to Susan's house.

The pair enjoyed their meal together, then set to work on the envelope stuffing.

"You've got a couple of extra inserts this week. I hope you're getting more money for this job?"

Susan assured her friend she was and how grateful he could give her a start.

Susan and Alan worked till late that night, and eventhough the young woman wanted to talk about Alan's cross-dressing, she kept her thoughts to herself.

Over the next few weeks, eventhough Alan helped her once or twice a week, Susan felt that Alan was becoming distant with her. Noticing that the young man rarely shaved, she sometimes noticed that Alan hadn't washed his hair.

'Alan is always proud of his hair and how it looked.' So said the young woman to herself.

"Hello, Janet." Said Susan to the woman just leaving Alan's home. "Is Alan all right? He seems preoccupied and doesn't seem to be looking after himself properly."

"I think, Susan, that Alan is worried about something, but he won't talk to Mum, me, or Eleanor. When we ask him what the matter is, he just says he's tired. Alan does what he has to, and as you know, he comes over to your place. Hasn't he said anything to you?"

Susan now thought she knew what was wrong, but she couldn't tell Janet. Susan had promised never to mention Alan's cross-dressing to anyone, but now she knew his family was worried.

"I'll have a talk to Alan the next time he comes to my place. I'll let you know if I learn anything."

Janet thanked her neighbour and started off down the road. Just then, Eleanor appeared at the door. She saw Susan and asked.

"Did you see Janet leaving?"

"I've just been talking to her. She has only just gone around that corner."

Susan pointed to the left corner, and Eleanor trotted after her sister. Susan returned home and vowed to have a word with Alan.

A couple of days later, when Alan was helping Susan, the young woman said:

"Please don't take offence, Alan, but everyone, including me, is worried about you. You seem to be letting yourself go."

"What are you on about. I'm fine. Just a little tired, that's all."

"That is not all, Alan. Your hair is matted and greasy, and you haven't shaved today. Your mum and sisters are worried that something is wrong. Will you tell me what the problem is, or shall I tell you?"

"JUST SHUT UP, WILL YOU?" Alan shouted. "Do you want my help, or don't you?"

"Yes, I want your help, Alan, but something is wrong, and I think I can guess what it is."

"I'm not here to talk about me. I'm here to help you if you want me to, but I'm not staying where I'm not wanted." Alan rose from his seat at the table and started for the door.

Susan ran to the boy and pleaded with him.

"Please don't leave like this, Alan. You're hurting; I can see that. Why won't you talk to me about it?"

"I've nothing to say. Now let's get on with this work."

By ten o'clock, Alan decided to go home. The young man went straight to his bedroom and laid on his bed. That night the young man couldn't even be bothered to undress for bed. Then the following morning, Alan rose, cooked his mother's and his sisters' breakfast, ate nothing himself, went to the garden shed, and got on with his work.

Susan and Alan worked alone for the next few weeks, each working late into the night; sometimes, Alan worked all night.

Alan and Susan never spoke or visited each other. Alan, however, knew that Susan had been in touch with his mother by telephone.

The summer came and went, and Christmas was on the horizon. Martin had called on his friend and was surprised by Alan's appearance. Alan hadn't been to the Rock and Roll club for months.

Susan wanted to tell Alan's mother what she thought the problem was but was afraid of permanently alienating her friend. Susan knew, though, that something must be done to save her friends sanity.

Christmas passed, and the new year was about to start. The Rock and Roll club had advertised a 'NEW YEARS EVE PARTY.

"Are you going to the party, Alan?" Asked Janet and Eleanor.

"Not this year. I don't feel in the party mood." Janet said:

"Look, mum is getting about now. I know she can't use the stairs yet. So you can go out and not worry."

"I've just said I'm not in the mood for parties."

The twins shrugged their shoulders, Called a "cheery see you later." To their mother, and left the house.

Susan caught the girls and asked if Alan was going to the Rock and Roll party.

"He doesn't even want to go to that."

Susan returned home. Sitting in her kitchen with a mug of tea, the young woman stared across the road to Alan's house. Then Silently to herself, Susan said:

'My new year's resolution is to tell Alan's mother why Alan is so low at the moment. I have to save the boy from himself.' Susan smiled to herself; now she had to make a plan.

"I just need to get, Mrs. Berry...Sorry, Sheila alone in the house. I'll explain the pain and torment that Alan suffers. She's already often said what a great son he is."

Susan was sure that the boy's mother would understand, and she then started to prepare herself for the interview. Then a little later that evening, Susan wondered if she was doing the right thing. Nearly changing her mind, Susan convinced herself that she was right.

"Just a couple of days to go." Said Susan aloud.

CHAPTER TEN

Susan had to find an excuse to get Alan out of his house. Susan wasn't sure what she could do. The young woman worked away for a while, then she thought about how Alan had organised his work. Susan had a garage, but unlike the garage at the Berry house, hers was at the bottom of the garden and contained her little red estate car.

'What can I do?' The woman asked herself. Then she came up with a plan. Not a very good plan, but a plan nonetheless.

Going over to Alan's house and knocking on the door, Susan was surprised to see Sheila Berry at the door.

"Come in, Susan. Do you want to talk to Alan?"

"I would, yes. I have a job I'm hoping he can help me with."

Sheila called her son and, after a minute, received no answer.

"That's odd. I thought Alan was at work in the shed."

"I'll go and look. Maybe he is concentrating on his paperwork."

Susan returned to tell the boy's mother that he wasn't in the shed. Then Susan said:

"Shall I take a look in his room?"

"I think you had better, Susan. I still can't manage the stairs."

After the simple directions, Susan went to her friend's bedroom. The door was locked. Susan banged on the door and called Alan, but she received no answer. She hammered harder and again only got silence.

"Alan must be out. He has locked his door." Called the young woman from the top of the stairs.

"There isn't a lock on his door." Sheila had panic in her voice. Susan tried knocking again but with no luck.

"Shall I force the door?"

The sound of voices in the kitchen delayed an answer to the question.

"What's going on?" So said the twins. Sheila said:

"Alan seems to have locked himself in his room." It was Janet who raced to the top of the stairs and she to banged on her brother's bedroom door.

"ALAN! ALAN! Is there something wrong?"

There was still silence from the far side of the door. Finally, Eleanor called the two women.

"Force the door; Alan might be ill."

Together, Janet and Susan put their shoulders to the door and pushed. Nothing happened, so they tried again. There seemed to be no movement of the door. Then Susan suggested rushing the door. The two girls stood a little away from the door, there wasn't much room to manoeuvre, but they did what they could. Then the girls rushed at the door. The sound of splintering wood could be heard from the foot of the stairs, and the two young women were thrust into the room.

The young man they had been trying to rouse was lying on his bed, fully clothed and unconscious. Although Janet was first at the boy's bedside, and she tried to lift his head, it was a dead weight.

Eleanor arrived at the top of the stairs, and as she did, both sisters called their brother's name. Susan checked Alan's pulse and announced.

"He's still alive! What has he done?"

As Janet laid her brother's head back on the pillow, she saw on his bedside cabinet a few white pills. Neither she nor her sister could read what they were as their eyes were blinded by tears. Susan picked up the packet.

"What's going on? Is Alan alright? Someone speak to me, please." Sheila was frantic for a reply, and Susan called to the boy's mother.

"Telephone for an ambulance... Quick as you can."

Susan now had the job of trying to calm down Janet and Eleanor. She had managed to read what was on the pill box and discovered that Alan had swallowed a quantity of painkillers.

They heard the ambulance's siren as it approached the cul-de-sac a few minutes later.

After being told what appeared to have happened, the boy was rushed away to the hospital.

"You two go to the hospital. I'll stay with your mum. Just ring here as soon as you know anything."

Susan saw the sisters off as they went after their brother. Then Susan made sure that Sheila was comfortable and said:

"Would you like me to make you a cup of tea, Sheila?"

"I would prefer a large brandy, Susan. There's a bottle in the sideboard."

Susan looked about the room before Sheila said:

"Alan put the sideboard in my bedroom."

Susan found the brandy and the glasses. Then she heard Sheila call.

"I expect you could do with one as well."

Back in the lounge, Susan poured out two measures of brandy. Sheila watched as the young woman dispensed the beveridge, then said:

"Put a decent amount in the glasses. I know I need a decent drink. You're shaking, girl, so need a good measure as well."

The two women sat and drank their brandies in silence, staring at the telephone, willing it to ring with good news.

Sheila asked for a second glass of brandy, and Susan obliged before saying.

"Are you alright having alcohol with your medication?"

"To hell with my medication. I need this more." Sheila held up her glass to illustrate her statement.

"I'll go and check the door to Alan's room. I had better take that empty pill box away as well." Sheila didn't reply; she just swallowed a large mouthful of the warming liquid.

Looking about Alan's room, Susan looked at the damage to the door frame. Next, the young woman picked up the splintered wood and the pill box from the cabinet. As she tidied up, Susan saw a folded sheet of paper on the floor, which she retrieved and placed on the cabinet. She was about to turn away when she glimpsed through the thin paper the word SORRY. Susan wondered if she was being nosey. However, she opened the folded sheet and read the contents.

"Oh...My...God!" Susan couldn't believe what she had read. Refolding the note, Susan hurried back to the lounge, nearly falling down the stairs.

"Sheila...Sheila. You had better look at what I have found." Susan placed the letter into the older woman's shaking hand and took her glass from the other. Susan sat herself down as the boy's mother read the message. As she read, tears ran down her cheeks and dripped onto the paper.

CHAPTER ELEVEN

"Why would Alan leave a note like this? What has he done to be sorry for?"

Susan could guess, but now was not the time to explain. The woman wasn't herself. She had been in hospital and was now at home but was still experiencing pain and seemed intoxicated. Sheila handed the message to Susan. The woman picked up her glass a sipped, but the glass was empty. Then holding the glass towards the young woman, Sheila said:

"Could you pour me another?"

"I think you've had enough, Sheila."

"I need another, and if you don't get it for me, I'll get it myself."

Susan hated what was happening to the woman. Susan wasn't sure it was safe for Sheila to consume so much alcohol.

"I'll make you a coffee, Sheila. You are going to make yourself ill. I'll make the coffee, and we will wait to hear from Janet and Eleanor."

Sheila knew her young friend was right and apologised for her behaviour. Sheila sat silently reading the note while she waited for her coffee.

'I love you, mum, and you, Janet and Eleanor. I have lived with a terrible secret that I can't explain but can't go on. I am truly sorry for what I am about to do; I want you to know that it has nothing to do with any of you. Please tell Susan that I love her dearly and thank her for her help. Remember. I always love you all.

Alan XXXX

SORRY

Susan entered the lounge and found Sheila sobbing. Susan said nothing. She gently pulled the note from the woman's fingers, folded it, and placed it on the telephone table. The two women sipped their hot coffee and silently waited for news of Alan and his condition.

It was pretty dark outside, and Susan started to close the curtains.

"No, Susan. Don't shut out the night." The woman's voice croaked as she spoke. "It's taking a long time to hear from the hospital. I hope they have sorted my son out. My lovely son."

The woman wept again.

Susan remained silent; she decided to let the woman talk if she wanted to. There had to be a time that she could reveal her friend's secret, but it wasn't yet. Sitting in the silence of that lounge, Susan thought back to the first time that Alan had stayed, and he had worn that nightie of hers. Alan was so happy that night that she couldn't believe he had tried to take his own life.

The room's silence was almost deafening, and when the telephone rang, it made the two women jump. Grabbing the phone, Susan said:

"Hello...Just a minute, I'll hand the phone over to her."

Handing the instrument to Sheila, Susan listened and watched as the woman's face changed every few seconds. Susan couldn't read her friend's face.

"Yes...Yes...I understand. Yes...Yes...Will he be all right?...When can he come home? I see. Thank you....If you wouldn't mind. Bye."

Susan could tell that one of the woman's daughters was speaking to her. Sheila smiled a weak smile and replaced the receiver after a few minutes. Then Sheila looked at the young woman by her side and said:

"Alan's going to be alright." The women hugged and laughed and sighed and then laughed some more. "They will keep him in for a few days to make sure, but the doctor thinks they got everything out of him. Alan was sleeping when the girls spoke to me, and they are on their way back home.

Susan cried as she took the coffee cups to the kitchen to replenish them. She was going to have to talk to Alan when he was home. It was crunch time, and his mother and sisters had to be told what was wrong. Susan had decided to give Alan an ultimatum. If he didn't tell them, then she would. But, she wasn't prepared to lose her friend because of his need to wear female attire.

It wasn't long before the twins arrived home. Susan offered to make them coffee, but when they saw the brandy bottle, that was what they needed, so they said.

"Why do you think he did it or was it an accident? So asked Janet.

Sheila passed the note to Janet, and Eleanor read it over her sister's shoulder. The girls read the letter twice, handed it back to their mother, then after a moment of silence, together they said:

"What terrible secret could he have? Alan doesn't do anything that would get him into trouble."Then Janet said:

"Alan hasn't even pinched a few sweets from a shop. I know most of his friends have at one time or another. Even we've done that. Haven't we, Eleanor?" Janet then realised what she had just said.

"Girls! You haven't?"

"Sorry, mum, but when we were Alan's age, we had done it a couple of times. All our friends had. Most kids try it, mum. I expect if you were honest, you would admit to doing it yourself. I know dad did. He did to us what his dad did to him. We got a clout. Why do you think dad stopped our pocket money that time?"

Sheila was horrified by her daughter's revelation, and she pointed out that she was shocked that her husband had admitted to such a thing to his children, but they had been punished.

"I would like to point out that according to you, Alan and I are unusual," Sheila looked at Susan, who raised her palms defensively and told everyone that she also was innocent. "as Susan also appears to be."

Everything settled down, and Janet asked her mother if she would like another brandy. The woman glanced across at Susan and then said to her daughter.

"I think I've had enough for one night." Susan and Sheila then grinned at each other.

"It's late now. I need to get some sleep. I'll come over early tomorrow and finish some of Alan's work."

"You don't need to do that, Susan. You have your own work to complete."

"Alan has helped me loads of times; I'm only returning his kindness."

Suppose Susan could get some of the stuff into the lounge in the morning. Show her what to do. Sheila offered to help as well.

"It'll give me something to do and take my mind off Alan." And so it had been settled—mother and friend would see that Alan completed his assignment on time.

<h1 style="text-align:center">CHAPTER TWELVE</h1>

Susan and Sheila worked their socks off to get all of Alan's assignment complete. Susan worked all; through the night and completed the whole job. Finally, everything was in the garage, awaiting the van to arrive in a couple of days.

"Can you get some of your stuff over here, and I'll help with your envelope stuffing. Is that what it's really called, Susan?"

"Yes, Sheila, it really is. Are you sure you can help?"

"Susan, look at what you have done, and the girls have offered to help when they get home from work. You only have a couple of days to have everything ready."

With everything settled, Susan's work was completed. Then, the van arrived, loaded the finished jobs, and unloaded the next assignment.

Later that day, Sheila and Susan was surprised when Alan unexpectedly arrived home.

"Alan! How did you get here?" Asked the boy's mother. "Taxi, mum. I just have to go and get my wallet and pay the driver."

"I'll do that." Susan dashed out the front door and soon returned full of smiles. Susan could see that the young man was pale looking. She took the young man in her arms and hugged

95

him and kissed him full on the lips and, in so doing, caused a lot of colour to appear on the boy's cheeks.

"Are you okay, Alan?" Said the boy's mother as she took hold of her son.

"I'm fine, Mum. I really am. And I am very sorry to cause you all a lot of trouble. I didn't think." Alan dropped to his knees, buried his face in his mother's lap, and cried freely. Then, with her hand on his head, the boy's mother comforted him.

As Susan departed, Janet and Eleanor arrived home. The girls were overjoyed to see their bother back home. Sheila offered to cook something for their tea, but Janet had a better idea.

"Eleanor, phone Susan and ask her what she likes from the Chinese takeaway. Then sort out what mum and Alan want, and I'll go and get it.

"What about me? You haven't asked me what I want."

"I know what you want. You'll have the same as me as you always do. Or do you want something else?" The room was quiet for a few moments, then Eleanor said:

"I'll have whatever you're having."

Even. Alan had to laugh.

Eleanor called Susan, and an hour later, everyone sat in the dining room eating a hot Chinese meal, all thanks to Janet.

Alan thanked everyone for doing his work for him and how they had all helped Susan.

It took about a week before things had settled back to normal. Alan's mum was getting about a lot better, and she had started cooking for everyone again. First, however, she had to have help with the cleaning, and as Alan said:

"That's why I work from home now. So I can help around the house and I don't mind taking a turn with the cooking."

The weather had turned, and the days were slowly getting longer; Alan had started to help Susan with her job, and the couple would work late into the night.

One evening after, Alan had tea at Susan's, and they settled down to the task of stuffing envelopes. Susan said:

"Why did you do it?"

"Do what?"

"You know what, Alan. I'm not going to say it."

Alan was silent, his brow furrowed, deep in thought, and Susan wasn't going to break the spell.

"I had had enough, Susan. I don't want to be sent to some mental institution, but now I realise I don't want to die either."

Susan leant across the table, took the boy's hands in hers, and started to explain something.

"Look, Alan. When I get up in the morning, sometimes I fancy wearing a skirt or a dress, but other times I want to wear trousers or jeans. Do you think I should be sent to a mental hospital?"

"Well, no, but you are a woman. So you are allowed to wear what you want. Men have to wear trousers. It's the law."

"Well, that's rubbish. You've seen men wearing kilts, haven't you? A kilt is just a skirt. I want to explain something to you, but first, I want to go and get a book I borrowed from the library."

Alan was nervous as he waited for Susan's return. He wondered what this book could be about. Then the young woman arrived back with the book. Then sitting next to her friend, she opened the book and showed the boy a picture of some Roman soldiers.

"Look, Alan. They are wearing skirts. Susan turned to another part of the book and showed the young man some men from Asia, and again she turned to another section of the book, where more men were wearing dress-like clothes.

"As you can see, men have worn dresses and skirts in the past. But, there's something else you should know. It took women a long time before they were accepted to wear trousers. So, if you look at it right, you could say you are ahead of your time. I've also discovered that there are many boys and men just like you. I've discovered a group called: The Beaumont

Society. If you want to, you can get in touch with them. They will, I am sure, be able to help you."

"Thank you, Susan, but I think I might be over all that now."

The young woman put her arm around her friend's shoulder. She appeared to be happy for the young man, but she felt that Alan was in denial.

"Let's get back to work. I would like to ask you one thing, though. If you don't mind?"

Alan looked a little worried, then the girl said:

"You don't have to answer me if you don't want, but," The girl paused before continuing. "when you were dressing in Eleanor's clothes. Did you want to be a girl?"

"No. I still wanted to be a boy, I suppose. Being a girl hadn't entered my head. I just felt so relaxed and comfortable in a dress or skirt. That night you gave me the nightie and knickers to wear was fantastic. I felt really great and what you did to me was unbelievable. I had never experienced anything like that."

"Would you go to bed with me again? No nightie this time."

Alan grasped the woman's hands and told her he loved her and would go to bed with her.

"I would like you to teach me how to make you feel like I felt that night."

It was arranged that Alan would call over the following evening, and when they had done enough work, they would sleep together.

"I'll have to let Beryl know you are staying over, but she won't disturb us. I think she might even be pleased, in her own way."

So it had been settled. Their work continued until they were too tired to do more, and Alan returned home.

Alan explained to his mother that he would stay with Susan that night. Sheila was fine about her son's arrangement. Susan was a sensible girl, and she trusted her son.

Susan and Alan got little work done that night. Then, in bed, Susan saw to it that Alan had the experience he had enjoyed before, and then she started to instruct the young man on how to please a woman.

Then the couple showered together and dried and powdered each other. Alan looked a little worried.

"What's wrong, Alan?"

"Are you sure I did everything alright?"

"You were great, Alan. And with time, you will get better and better. I have enjoyed our exquisite night. Let's get to bed; I don't know about you, but I need some sleep."

The young couple slept naked that night, not waking until mid-morning. Eventhough it was an overcast day, the sun shone brightly on Alan. So was this to be a new faze of the young man's life.

CHAPTER THIRTEEN

Work had to be completed, so the young couple helped each other. Alan's mother wanted something to occupy her as she sat in her chair in the lounge, and Susan provided the distraction. Susan and Alan would work together in Alan's shed while Sheila worked in the lounge. The system they had was sound.

"I want to try and get upstairs, Alan." Said Sheila. "It's been months since I have seen my bedroom."

Alan agreed but told his mother that he would follow close behind, just in case she fell.

"This is more difficult than I had expected." Said the boy's mother as she stepped a little further up the staircase.

"Come down, mum. You're not ready yet. I can't leave trying to climb the stairs."

The young man held onto his mother's waist as he guided her back to the bottom of the stairs.

"You need to talk to the doctor again and see if there is anything we can do to help you."

Alan hadn't realise how frustrated his mother was getting with her immobility. The woman would get angry with herself, and after her trials at the stairs, she found she had to rest for some time, which meant that Alan had to prepare the meals, which made Sheila more depressed.

"Look, mum, I don't mind. I keep telling you that I gave up work to look after you. Anyway, I still earn money."

"It's your birthday soon. But, unfortunately, I haven't been able to get out and buy you anything. Not even a birthday card."

"Mum, I don't need anything; I want you to get better and be happy."

The woman touched her son's cheek and caressed it, then said:

"You're a good boy, Alan. I'll telephone the doctor and see when he can call round to see me."

Alan went to the kitchen and started dinner. Susan put her head around the kitchen door.

"Everything alright, Alan?"

The boy explained what had been happening with his mother.

"I won't be able to come over tonight. I need to be here for mum in case the doctor calls."

"Is there anything I can do to help?"

There wasn't much for Susan to do, and after Alan had explained, he told the young woman that he had a lot on his plate and would call over to her place as soon as he could.

It wasn't to be until the following afternoon that Doctor Kelsey arrived. Then sitting in the lounge with Sheila, Alan could hear the doctor explain to the boy's mother that she shouldn't be trying the stairs yet.

"Hasn't anyone explained to you, Mrs. Berry. You are to have a hip replacement, but when you fell you have done some damage to your hip. We have to wait until your injury has healed before the operation can occur. I will arrange for you to have an X-ray. You will also have to have hospital transport to get you there."

"Have you any idea how long before I get this appointment, doctor?"

"It shouldn't be too long, Mrs. Berry. I have made a note that it is very urgent. Do you have anyone who can accompany you on the day?"

Alan walked in through the open door and said:

"I can go with mum. I work here at home, so there is no problem."

The doctor seemed happy and left mother and son while he travelled to his next patient.

Susan had seen the doctor arrive and then when she saw that he was leaving she went across the road to see how Sheila was. Sheila Berry looked disheartened as she told her young friend what the doctor had said.

"I can help as well. We don't want to leave everything to Alan. Jane and Eleanor have their work to do. They have to earn money to keep you all going. I know they understand." Sheila was broken hearted as she spoke.

"I need to earn some money like the others. Can you get me some of that envelope stuffing job you do? I won't be able to do what you and Alan manage, but every little will help. I do miss my cleaning job so much."

Susan promised that she would see what she could do. Alan arrived with two mugs of tea for the ladies, then continued with the dinner preparations.

Susan popped into the kitchen with the empty mugs. The young woman kissed her friend on the lips and left.

Over the next couple of weeks, Susan would call across to see how Alan and Sheila were getting along. Then one morning, Sheila told Susan.

"My appointment has come through. I will be seen on Monday." The woman was solemn as she spoke.

"But, that's good news, isn't it?"

"I'm worried about Alan. He spends most of his time in the shed or his room. He eats little, if anything, and even Janet and Eleanor have noticed. I showed him this letter, "The woman illustrated her statement by waving it. "all he could say was that it was good that they have got in touch."

"Would you like me to talk to, Alan? He might tell me if anything is wrong."

Sheila agreed and told the young woman where she could find Alan. The young woman mounted the stairs to Alan's bedroom. The door was jammed shut. Then it hit the girl. Deja-vu. She had been here before.

"Oh, no. Alan! Alan! Can you hear me?" The girl hammered on the door. Then a voice called from the bottom of the stairs.

"What's up, Susan. Is something wrong?"

The young woman nearly fell down the stairs as she saw Alan's face peering up at her.

"Where were you, Alan?"

"Out in the shed, working."

"Your mum said that you were in your bedroom. Anyway, your door jammed shut again. I thought....."

"The door sticks since it was repaired. I need to get some money for the carpenter to come and fix it."

Susan hugged her friend. She was pleased he was safe.

"That's good about your mum's appointment, isn't it?"

Alan was almost dismissive with his reply in the affirmative.

"Are you all right, Alan? You seem distant for some reason."

Alan assured the girl he was fine, and after she had offered to listen to him if he wanted to talk, she went home.

Alan stayed away from Susan for a few days, that is, until the day his mother had to go for her X-ray.

Alan said nothing about it being his birthday, he wanted it to pass unnoticed.

"Sorry to trouble you, Susan, but would you mind running me to the hospital? Mum has to have her X-ray today, and the ambulance has just arrived to collect her. I thought I could go with them, but they have other patients to pick up."

"Of course, I will, Alan. I said I wanted to help. Come through, and we'll get the car out."

Alan waited outside the garage as Susan drove her little red estate car from the garage. Then, finally, Alan closed the door, and the two set off for the hospital.

"Susan, you said I could talk to you. Do you mind listening to me as we drive?"

"I think I know what you want to tell me. Do you want me to start?"

Alan nodded, then realised that the young woman wouldn't have seen what he had done. However, out of her eye, she saw the boy silently saying yes.

Susan waited before speaking. Then she said:

"It's all starting up again, isn't it?"

Alan had trouble speaking and had to clear his throat first. Then saying yes, he started to cry. Susan pulled the car to the side of the road. Then, switching the engine off, the young woman turned and looked directly at the boy.

"How long?"

"Several weeks now."

"And you have told no one?"

"No."

"This time, Alan, you have no choice."

"I know, but I am petrified."

The young man was shaking so much that Susan could feel the car shaking. Finally, the young woman took the boy's hand from his lap and held it before saying.

"Would you like me to be with you?"

"I would, Susan. I'm sorry to burden you with this, but I have no one else I can turn to."

Without letting go of her friend's hand, Susan kissed the boy's cheek and said:

"Let's get to the hospital."

Sheila Berry ended up staying at the hospital all day. Susan kept Alan company while he stayed with his mother. Sheila was cheerful after her day of being pushed about the hospital.

"I thought I just had an X-ray, but I have seen various specialists, and it looks like things are moving along."

Two ambulance men arrived to wheel Sheila to her transport and then home.

In the car, Alan said to Susan.

"I want to do this tonight when we get home."

Susan agreed, and it wasn't long before Susan was putting her car away.

The young couple walked across the street hand in hand and entered Alan's home. Janet and Eleanor were making their evening meal. Janet said:

"Hello, you two. Are you staying to eat with us, Susan?"

"I would like that very much, Janet. Thank you." As they ate, they chatted aimlessly about various things; Alan said that he would wash up as the girls had cooked the meal. After their meal, Janet and Eleanor started for the stairs. Alan said:

"Can we all go to the lounge? I have something to tell you."

"I bet he's been promoted." Said Eleanor. Janet's reply to that remark was.

"Don't be silly; you don't get a promotion in Alan's type of work."

Alan was the last to enter the lounge; Sheila had remained silent; she had a worried look.

Alan waited until everyone, including Susan, sat down. Janet and Eleanor sat on their mother's bed. Alan just stood in the doorway.

"Well! What's this news you have for us?" Asked the twins.

"Alan will tell us in his own good time," Sheila said, still looking worried. His mother's mind had wandered to when Alan had taken the overdose of painkillers. Alan started to speak, his mouth opened but nothing would come out. Then he tried again.

"Mum, Janet, Eleanor. I'm not sure how to start." Alan said. His mother started to cry. Alan couldn't speak with his mother, tears falling from her cheeks.

 Susan got up, went to the boy's side, and took his hand. This action seemed to give Alan some courage.

"Mum...Girls...I...Er...Er...I like to wear... dresses and skirts." Alan had blurted out those last words, then cried.

Susan put her arm around the boy's shoulders. There was silence in the room. The silence lasted for a minute, then Janet and Eleanor started to laugh.

"Okay! What's the gag?"

Sheila just sat silently and stared at her son. The girls continued laughing.

"Come on, what is it you wanted to tell us." Janet insisted."

Alan was red-faced as he repeated himself.

"I sometimes like to wear a dress or a skirt. I have been like this for a few years."

The girls stopped laughing, and Eleanor said:

"He's serious."

The boy's mother still remained silent. Instead, she just stared at her son.

"Mum, say something. Anything, but please say something."

It was Eleanor who spoke.

"Where have you got these dresses and skirts from, and where are they now?"

"I'm sorry that I borrowed your things, Eleanor."

"Which of my clothes did you borrow?"

"I have worn your pink party dress, the grey one that looks a bit like a school dress, and the green pleated skirt."

"My, God." Eleanor was silent for a few seconds before she said. "I'll have to get them and burn them. I can't wear them now that some pervert has had them on."

Alan burst into tears, and Susan held him tight. The young woman was horrified at the boy's sister's reaction. Susan was about to say something when Sheila spoke for the first time.

"You're going to need some sort of therapy. I'll have to get on to doctor Kelsey. He'll know the best psychiatrist."

Janet stared at her brother, then at Susan.

"How long have you known about our perverted brother?"

"Alan is not a pervert. Lots of men and boys sometimes feel the need to wear a dress. Alan has held this from you because he was afraid you would react as you have." Looking into Alan's eyes, she continued. "You were right, Alan. I should never have made you tell your family. They always praised you, and I genuinely thought that they would understand. I was wrong."

Alan went over to his mother, and as he got close, she said:

"Keep away from me. You're sick in the head." Janet said:

"I know he says he's only worn yours and hasn't worn them, but I'll get rid of the same stuff that he has used of yours."

"I think you are all sick. Yes, Alan was wrong to borrow your clothes, Eleanor, he should have said something before, but he was afraid you would react the way you have. Look what Alan has done for you. Especially you, Sheila. Alan gave up work, rearranged the house for you and you two," Susan pointed at the twins. "Alan has cooked your meals, done the washing, and kept the house clean. You don't deserve a brother or son like Alan."

"We don't want him here. You will have to find somewhere else to live." Said Sheila." Susan pulled Alan away from his mother; the boy was crying uncontrollably. Susan pulled her friend to the door when through his tears, Alan said:

"What about my work. I'll have to find somewhere to move it to."

"Don't worry about that for now, Alan. You had better come over to my house."

"Thanks, Susan. I know you care."

Alan was still crying when the couple left the house. However, once inside Susan's place, the boy started to calm down a little. Susan poured out a couple of large brandies, then the young woman apologised to her friend.

"The way your mum always praised you. She often told me what a kind and considerate boy you were. I never believed she would turn on you like that. Janet and Eleanor are of your generation, and I thought they would accept the way you are. Alan. You can stay here as long as you want to. You can have the spare room as your own. I'll have to tell Beryl about you. You won't mind, will you?"

"I don't care anymore. Beryl won't be any worse than my own family."

Susan and Alan had a second brandy. Alan was shaking, and so Susan took the boy in her arms and hugged him before kissing him on the lips. It was a long, lingering kiss.

"Beryl will be home at her usual time. We'll tell her together. Now go and have a sleep on my bed. I'll call you when I'm getting tea ready."

As the young man climbed the stairs with a heavy heart, he tried to picture Beryl's reaction. 'Would she want him banished from her home as well?'

Alan laid down on the bed and slowly drifted off to sleep. Unbeknownst to the young man, Susan looked in on her slumbering friend.

CHAPTER FOURTEEN

The young man on Susan's bed was sleeping soundly when she went to wake him. Susan was surprised that he slept at all. 'It must have been all the worrying and the tension that has made him so tired.'

"Alan! Alan! I'm just getting tea ready."

Slowly the boy sat up. He rubbed his eyes and stared at the woman standing by his side. He looked around him and saw that he was in Susan's bedroom.

"So it's true, is it?"

"I'm afraid it is, Alan."

"Come down, and I'll make a cup of tea. Beryl will be home soon.

Alan ran his fingers through his hair and followed the woman down the stairs to the kitchen.

Susan made a pot of tea, and the pair sat at the table and drank as they waited for the arrival of Beryl. Alan's stomach churned as the time approached, and his heart beat faster. The young man could feel the sweat seeping from his brow.

They heard the front door open. Beryl walked into the kitchen as she removed her coat.

"Hello, Alan. Susan looking after you, I hope?"

Alan said that she was then shut his mouth.

"If you don't mind? Alan is going to have the spare room for now."

"I don't mind if you don't. The room will have to be cleared a bit. That bed will have to be cleared off and then made up. I'll do some of it if you like. When we've had something to eat. I'm going out a little later tonight."

Beryl left the kitchen to hang up her coat and change her shoes. Alan could hear the woman upstairs.

"She didn't even ask why I need a room here."

"Don't worry, Alan. I'll do all the talking."

Beryl was soon back in the kitchen.

"Cor! That's better. Those shoes have been playing my feet up nearly all day. Now. Tell me. Why do you need a room here?"

"Alan has been nursing a secret for some time. I pleaded with him to tell his mum and sisters, but it backfired, and he's been thrown out."

"Before Susan could continue, Beryl said:

"Don't tell me. So Alan is homosexual, and his family is horrified?"

"Not really, Beryl. Alan is a cross-dresser."

Susan then remained silent, waiting for a reply, and Alan held his head down, waiting for the explosion.

"Is that all? I'm sorry, Alan, but I think there's something wrong with your family."

Alan looked up at Beryl. His tears were apparent. Then after the silence, Beryl smiled, then said:

"Well, do we eat? We have a room to get ready."

Alan took a little time to adjust to his situation, and after they had eaten, Beryl was the first to start work on what was to become Alan's room.

Alan wanted to do the washing up, but Susan told him to go and give, Beryl a hand.

In the spare room, Beryl was first clearing the bed. Then she said:

"I think there's some stuff in that wardrobe. We can probably dump most of it."

As the pair worked, they discovered that there wasn't as much as Beryl and her sister had first thought. Susan came to help, and everything that could be boxed was boxed, and the room was habitable.

"After I have made the bed, Alan, you'll be able to come up here whenever you want to. We'll get the rest of the stuff out as soon as possible. The dustman will take some." Susan was smoothing out the duvet and checking that everything was okay. Beryl then said:

"Did you bring any clothes with you?"

"No. I just have what I'm wearing." Beryl said:

"Don't worry, I'll go over and get you a change of clothes."

"My bedroom door sticks, it feels as if it is locked, but if you give it a good shove, it'll open. There is a case on my wardrobe. Thank you very much, Beryl. You're great."

"Don't be daft. There's a fellow at our office. He's a cross-dresser. He thinks we don't know, but sometimes his bra shows through his shirt. There are lots of blokes just like you."

Beryl was soon back. The woman was carrying the case that Alan had indicated. Susan said:

"You can wash anything as you need to. But, first, I'll show you how to work the machine."

"You two are unbelievable. I love you both."

Alan then kissed Susan on the lips and Beryl on the cheek.

"Shuck's, Alan." Beryl caressed her cheek. Then she said:

"What about dresses and skirts. You'll want something to change into.

Alan couldn't believe his ears. Finally, two women accept him as he truly is. These two women are even preparing to supply his needs.

"I don't know how to thank you both. I could never have thought that I would be here like this in my wildest dreams. I wish my mum and sisters could accept me like you two." Beryl said:

"I have to go out in a little while. Before I jump in the bath, you had better come with me, Alan."

The young man wondered what Beryl had in store for him. Beryl and Alan went into the woman's bedroom, where Beryl went over to the large wardrobe. She slid open the door on the left and said to Alan.

"From here to here," Beryl pointed out what she meant." I haven't worn any off this stuff for a long time. So take a look, and if you like something, you can just take it."

Alan was frozen to the spot staring at dresses and skirts. Then Beryl broke the boy's silence when she said:

"Here, this should fit you," Beryl pulled a pale blue plain-looking dress from the wardrobe, and she handed it to Alan." and so will this." Again the young woman gave the boy a garment. "Now go to your room and try them on."

Alan was red-faced as he left Beryl's bedroom and went to the spare room. Alan removed his shirt and trousers and put the blue dress on. The soft material felt pleasing and cosy to the young man. Then he took the grey pleated skirt, which he tried on. Beryl had been right. Both garments fitted fine. Alan replaced his shirt and stood looking at himself in the mirror on the wardrobe door. Then carefully hanging up the dress, Alan took another look at himself.

"Alan! Are you going to be long?" Susan had called from the kitchen.

"I just have to put the things away that Beryl gave me. Then I'll be down."

"Alan, come down in whatever you are wearing. I want to see you in it."

Alan was nervous about being seen in a skirt. The young man had always dressed up in secret, and here was a woman waiting to see him in a dress or skirt. It took the young man a few minutes to pluck up the courage to leave the bedroom, but eventually, he did. Walking slowly down the stairs so as to delay the humiliation, Alan finally arrived at the kitchen.

"Oh, yes. Beryl's skirt fits you fine. I have a blouse that will go with that. Give me a second."

Susan disappeared to her room and soon returned with a white blouse; Alan saw that it was pretty plain but had a frilly collar.

"Here, change into this."

Alan took the blouse and was soon wearing it. Susan took the boy's shirt and dropped it into the laundry basket.

"That'll be washed by tomorrow." Said the woman. "Now, are you ready to get some work done?"

Alan followed his friend into the other room, lost for words. So the two friends started the envelope stuffing. As they worked, a face suddenly poked through the doorway.

"Are! you're wearing the skirt." Beryl entered and continued.

"Stand up and let me take a look," After a moment's perusal.

"It looks good on you, Alan, but we need to do something about shoes and that hair on your legs, but you look okay. Susan's old blouse fits well, I see. Right, you two, I'm off. Don't wait up; I'll probably be late."

Alan's face was still red for a time after; Beryl had left, but Susan ignored it, and the couple continued with their work.

"I'll have a chat with, Beryl tomorrow, and we'll get your work stuff over here. I'll need some help to get the shed emptied."

"Look, Susan. My mum said I could work over at her house if I didn't go inside. I can use the side gate, go straight to my shed, and work. You and Beryl have already done too much for me."

"Don't be daft. The shed is full of junk, and if you help me, we can take most of the stuff to the council tip. It might take a couple of trips, but that doesn't matter. Would you like a glass of wine?"

Alan accepted the offer of a glass of wine, and as the pair worked away that evening, they chatted aimlessly about anything apart from Alan's family.

Susan suddenly yawned.

"My word, Alan. Look at the time. I don't know about you, but I'm ready for bed."

"So am I. Thank you, Susan, for the use of a bedroom."

"Do you want to sleep with me or in your new room? The choice is yours. I won't be offended if you choose to sleep in your own room."

"If you don't mind, just tonight, do you mind if I sleep alone?"

"Of course not, Alan. I was just giving you a choice. Come with me."

Alan followed the young woman up the stairs to her room, where she gave Alan a knee-length night dress of pink satin and a matching pair of knickers.

"Here, these are yours. While you wash and get changed, I'll make us a hot chocolate, and I'll bring yours to your room."

Alan did as he had been asked, washed and changed into his own night dress, and then got himself into bed. A knock at the door told the boy that Susan had arrived with his hot drink.

"Come in, Susan!" Called the boy.

Susan entered and sat on the bed after placing a small tray on the upturned box by the boy's bed.

"Comfy?"

"I am, Susan. Very comfortable, thank you."

Susan kissed the boy on the lips, then said her good night, and then she was gone.

Alan laid back against the headboard with his hands behind his head, and the boy smiled to himself. It had been a long time since he had felt this happy.

CHAPTER FIFTEEN

The following morning, Alan rose; first, he dressed and went down to the kitchen. He had a bit of a search but found what he had been looking for. Then the young man started to cook breakfast. The smell began to waft its way up the stairs to the two slumbering women. As he worked away, Alan made a pot of tea and coffee.

"Morning, Alan." Beryl yawned. "Wearing trousers again?"

"Yes. Susan and I are going to sort your shed out."

"It's about time. The thing is full of junk. I don't think there is anything in there that we want."

"Morning, Alan, Beryl. You're not wearing a dress or skirt this morning?" Beryl answered for the boy.

"Alan tells me that you are going to clear the shed this morning; that's why he's wearing trousers."

"I see. Well, I have an old denim dress you can have if you want to wear it while we work." Said Susan.

"I would like that very much. Thank you."

The three chums ate their breakfast, thanks to Alan. Then it was just Susan, and the boy and Alan got to wear the denim dress. The dress was a little long but fine, as Susan had told the boy.

"You won't be flashing your underwear when you bend over."

Alan blushed. He was to do a lot of that for a while. As the young man had never ventured outside while dressed as a female, he felt self-conscious as he walked into the garden. With Susan's help, the young man soon settled into the job at hand.

"We'll box up everything we can, then load my car. I can lower the back seat, so we will get quite a lot in there."

Alan agreed, and the two of them set to work. Alan soon forgot he was wearing a dress; he was even happy going to the end of the garden and loading Susan's car.

"It'll take another trip to get rid of everything, Alan, but I think you had better get some trousers on, and we'll get this lot unloaded."

At the tip, the car was emptied quickly, then Susan said:

"We'll go into town first."

Susan drove into the car park, then to Alan's surprise, she removed her shoes.

"Here, Alan, try these on." The young woman handed the boy her black low-heeled shoes.

Alan removed his shoes and put his feet into Susan's shoes."

"My feet go in alright, but they are a little snug."

The young woman felt the boy's feet and then announced that he needed the next size. So then, after replacing their shoes, the two friends headed for the shoe shop. First, they visited the women's department, and Susan showed the boy various styles that she thought best, and Alan made his selection. Then as he went to pay, Susan said:

"These are my treat, it was your birthday a while ago, and we didn't celebrate it."

"You can't spend your money on me. I'll pay as long as you go to the till for me."

"I insist, Alan. Now shut up."

Alan could feel his cheeks burning as his friend paid for the black shoes. Alan was sure the woman behind the counter knew the shoes were for him as she smiled at him. Then in the car.

"Here, Alan. Wear your new shoes home."

Alan put on the shoes as Susan pulled the car out of the car park, then drove home. As Susan reverses the car into the garage, ready to load up a second time, Alan starts to remove the shoes.

"No, leave them on. They are comfortable, aren't they?"

"Very, thank you."

"Keep them on for now; why we load up, it will give you a chance to get used to them."

Alan wore his new shoes until they were ready to leave for a second run to the tip; as soon as they returned home, Susan told her friend to go and shower first, then to change into the dress that Beryl had given him. So Susan showered while Alan dressed.

"That looks great, Alan. Do you feel comfortable?"

"I do, Susan. Thank you."

The boy kissed his friend. Then a short time later, there was a knock at the front door. Susan peered out the kitchen window, then pulled back and told Alan to go to his room and wait.

"Hi, Susan. Is Alan here. I've just been over to his house. His mother told me he was over here. The woman seemed a bit strange if you ask me."

"Hello, Martin. Yes, Alan is staying here, but he's having a bath. We've just emptied the shed, and we got rather dirty."

"I won't stop then. I just called to see if he was going to the club tonight. I haven't seen him in ages. Since he left the office, I only see him on the odd occasion."

"Are you sure you don't want to wait? I'm sure he won't be long."

"Just ask Alan if he could ring me if he's going to the club tonight. Thanks, Susan."

Susan watched and waited until Martin was out of the front garden and walking away, then she called Alan.

"You can come down now; Martin has gone," Susan continued as the boy descended the stairs. "and can you telephone him if you're going to the club tonight?"

"I'll go if you come with me?"

"What about your teddy boy outfit? Would you like me to go and get it for you?"

"Like I said. If you come with me, I'll go."

"In that case, you had better ring, Martin, and I'll get your clothes."

Susan left on her errand, and Alan waited. Susan returns very quickly.

"Your mum won't let me in. I think she blames me for what's happened."

"If you don't mind, we'll still go, but just for a couple of drinks; I can see my mates so they won't get suspicious."

Alan rang his friend, then when Beryl got home from work, she was informed that the two friends were off out for a little while.

"Before you go. I have something for you, Alan." Beryl handed over a parcel and said. "Happy birthday."

Alan, after thanking Beryl, opened the package. The young man found a couple of slips and a pack of knickers. There were also tights of various hues and a couple of pairs of stockings, a suspender belt, and a bra.

"I hope you like them, Alan. They should all fit, My dress and skirt fit you, so that was what I went by."

Alan hugged Beryl and kissed her. And he couldn't say thank you enough.

"Blimey!" Said Beryl. "It wasn't much."

"I've never worn anything like this before. I only ever just put a dress or skirt on. This is...Well...You know."

The girls knew.

"Enjoy your evening?" Said Beryl. Susan said:

"Your dinner is in the oven. It's ready when you are."

The couple left and had an enjoyable evening. Martin wanted to know what was wrong with Alan's mum, but Susan just said:

"Don't ask. It's a long story."

By the time the couple was nearly home, Susan had said:

"Do I get some company tonight?"

"Yes, you do. You've been so good to me about everything."

"Don't thank me. This was, in part, my fault. But shall we forget all that? You can be yourself whenever you like.

CHAPTER SIXTEEN

Alan joined Susan in her bed that night. He wore his nightie, but not for long. The couple enjoyed each other and fell asleep in each other's arms, waking early the following morning. Alan, after his shower, went to his room. There the young man took the bra and tried to put it on. Then he tried with the thing the wrong way round and fitted the bra into place across his chest.

Alan then put on a pair of his new knickers and one of the slips. The satin fabric felt great on his naked skin. Then the young man found it a little tricky getting into the tights but was soon ready to put on the blouse Susan had given him and then Beryl's grey skirt. Finally pushing his feet into his new shoes, the boy felt prepared to go to the kitchen.

"Morning, Susan. How do I look?"

"You look great, Alan. How do you feel?

"I don't think I have ever felt this good before."

"We'll do something about your hairy legs. But, first, I'll get you some hair remover."

"I can use my razor."

"No, you could cut yourself, and anyway, you'll quickly have stubbly legs. No hair remover is best. Oh, and I think we should get you a little padding for your bra. Your blouse will fit better then.

Alan's collection of female clothing slowly grew, thanks to Susan and her sister Beryl. Not only did they give the boy some of the clothes they no longer wore, but they bought Alan new things. Alan was now hairless all over, and his underclothes felt so good. Then one Sunday, while the three of them ate their Sunday roast, Beryl said:

"Would you like me to make you up next Sunday morning? Then as long as the weather is fine and you, Susan, don't mind, we could take a trip to the coast. If you drive Susan, I'll pay for the petrol and Alan you can spend the day as one of the girls. How does that sound?"

Alan didn't know what to say. Then almost as an afterthought, Alan said:

"But what about my hair?"

Susan and Beryl looked the boy over, then at each other.

"You'll have to shave off your sideburns, and I'll have to trim your hair a little, so on Saturday, I'll give you a perm and style your hair. What do you say, Alan?"

Nervously the boy agreed. He had doubts as to whether or not he would pass as female.

"Do you think you could do a good enough job on me, Beryl?" Susan said:

"She can. I promise you, you won't recognise yourself in the mirror when Beryl has finished with you."

So it was settled. The following weekend arrived, and Alan had already removed his sideburns. Beryl washed the boy's hair, and later that day, he had his curlers removed. Alan was pleased with his hair.

The day was a little cloudy, so Beryl, nearer to Alan's size, loaned the boy a waterproof jacket just in case of rain. Beryl also gave Alan a handbag to complete the illusion. Then with a bit of combing from Beryl and a copious amount of hair lacquer, the three were ready to depart.

They went to Susan's car through the garden, and with Alan next to Susan, they set off on the ninety-minute drive to the seaside.

The three of them sat on the beach for a while, Alan's eyes were darting about, and the girls could see that he was tense.

"You need to relax, Alan. No one is looking at you." Said Susan. Beryl announced she was getting hungry, so they left the beach and found a small restaurant.

"Alan, you must relax."

"We can't keep calling him Alan, Susan. Someone might hear. Alice, what about Alice?"

"Do you feel like an Alice?" Said Susan.

"I'll go along with whatever you say."

So it had been decided that Alan was now to be called Alice. She or her instead of him had also to be included. They had their meal, and Alan noticed that everyone in the restaurant was only interested in their own little worlds, and he started to relax.

The trio looked around the town, and it was time to head home. Halfway along their journey, they stopped at a little pub for a sandwich and a drink.

The day ended all too soon, but Alan had enjoyed himself. Finally, Alan was being the boy he wanted to be.

"I have to ask you, Alan, but have you ever wanted to be a girl. You know, have a sex change?" Asked Beryl.

"Never. I like being a boy. Well, I suppose I am a man now. I'm nineteen. I can vote. But no. I have always felt male. It's just the clothes. They make me feel relaxed and happy with myself."

Alan leant across to Beryl and squeezed her hand.

"I've had the best day ever. You two make every day fantastic."

Alan didn't wear any women's clothing the next day. He had his work to do in Susan and Beryl's, shed and, wearing his old jumper and jeans, the young man sat at his bench filling the sample boxes.

Over the coming months, Alan would sometimes be Alice, and at other times he was Alan. The young man had bought himself a new teddy boy outfit and each month he went and saw his mates at the club. Sometimes, Susan would accompany the young man, and at other times Beryl would join her sister and Alan.

It was more than a year since Alan had left home, and eventhough he only lived across the road, he rarely had sight of his mother or sisters.

Alan had decided to try and fix Susan and Beryl's front fence when.

"Hello, Alan." The stereo voice told Alan that his sisters were behind him.

"What do you want?"

"We want to see you, Alan. Can we talk to you?"

"If you want to."

Alan opened the front door and called Susan.

"Is it alright if my sisters come in for a moment?"

Susan was friendly to the two women; they all sat at the kitchen table. The girls were hoping to have Alan to themselves, but Alan was adamant that they had to talk in front of Susan.

The girls were sorry for what they had said and done. They hoped that their brother was happy.

"Mum wants to see you, you know?"

"She knows where I am."

"Mum feels rotten at the way she treated you."

"How does she think I felt? I probably wouldn't be around now if it wasn't for Susan and Beryl."

The girls had tears in their eyes as they tried to plead with the boy to go and see their mother.

"Has she had her operation yet?"

"Yes, but she has to walk with a stick."

"I'm sure she can walk over here."

The girls stood up and thanked their brother for listening to them, they thanked Susan for what she had done to look after their brother, and they left.

It took a week, but the young man's mother gave in and visited her son. She wanted to hug him but was unsure until Alan hugged his mother and told her to sit down. Mother and son cried.

Mrs. Berry asked her son to return home, but the boy pointed out that he was happy where he was.

"I can be myself, mum. No one criticises me." Susan had been silent during the exchanges over the past week, but she just had to speak up.

"Mrs. Berry. Sheila. I'm in love with your son. I know I am older than he is, but. And I haven't said this to Alan, but I want to marry him if he has me."

Beryl was pleased when she discovered that Alan had accepted her sister's proposal. She said that as soon as she could, she would find somewhere else to live as soon as they married, but that little problem was solved by Alan's mother and sisters. After the wedding, Beryl was to move across the street.

Things moved a little quicker than expected, but the big day arrived, and a handsome couple left the church, where Martin had been the best man for his lifelong friend.

Martin eventually discovered Alan's secret. He couldn't understand at first, but then, as time passed, Martin realised that Alan was still Alan. Nothing had changed between them.

I am nearing the end of the story of Alan but I have to say, that the young man was happy with his life. Mrs. Berry had gotten used to calling her son Alice whenever he was entirely made up and looked feminine. Other times Alan would just put on a dress or skirt like a woman and be happy as a man in a dress.

Beryl, Susan and Susan's husband, Mrs. Berry, and her two daughters would sometimes holiday together. Alan would be Alice a lot of the time but not all of it.

Susan and Alan are now pensioners with two wonderful girls and a boy. They also have seven grandchildren, and everyone accepts Alan for the man he really is.

I know Alan is happy with his life because, although I have changed the names because of those bigoted people.

I am Alan, and Susan is my wife of forty years. I hope this story has given you pleasure, and although different people have different reasons for cross-dressing, this is my tale.

I believe that in the not-too-distant future, men, boys, girls, and women will all be treated equally and, without fear, be able to wear whatever clothing they wish and feel comfortable wearing.

It has been stated many times that clothes have no gender; the labels that people put on them are the problem.

If you are a male who likes to cross-dress, let us hope that the day will come when you can live your life your way.

GOOD LUCK TO EVERYONE EVERYWHERE

NOT QUITE THE END